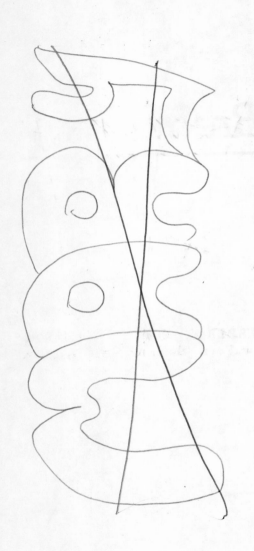

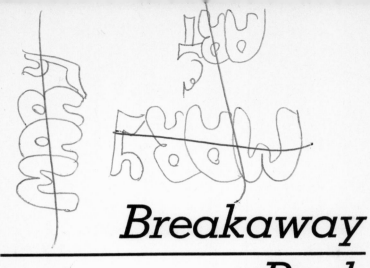

Breakaway
Back

by Nelson Hutto

HARPER & ROW, PUBLISHERS
New York, Evanston, and London

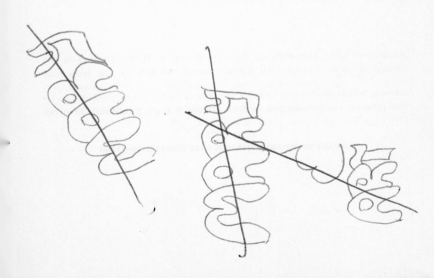

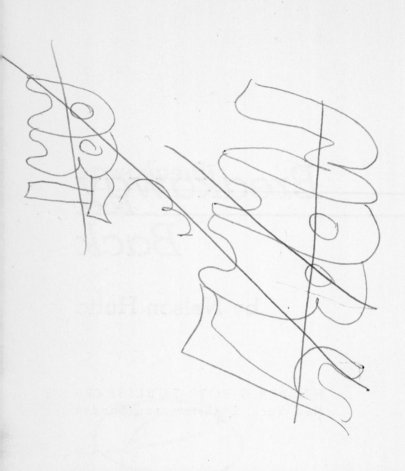

50

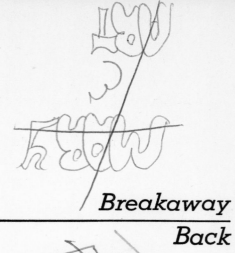

Breakaway

Back

134611

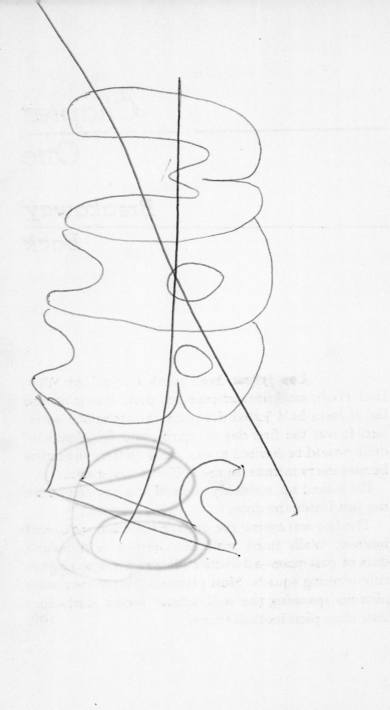

Chapter

One

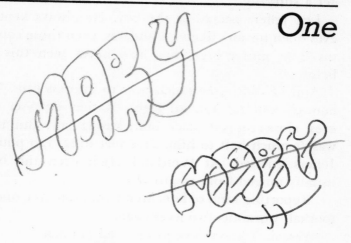

Lee Jeffers, head football coach at Westland High, sat hunched over his desk, intent on the list of tasks he'd jotted down for the afternoon workout. It was the first day of school, and from now on drills would be limited to one a day. Jeffers wanted to be sure every minute on the field was well spent.

He looked up, suddenly aware that a boy was standing just inside the door.

The boy was eyeing the walls of the office with awed interest. Walls lined with photographs of Westland stars of past years—all-district players, all-state players, title-winning squads. Most prominent were four large pictures spanning the wall behind Jeffers' desk—four state champion football teams.

"Anything I can do for you, son?"

Startled out of his concentration, the boy answered, "Yes, sir. I'm a student here. I came to see if I could get a suit."

Lee Jeffers peered at the boy. He always kept his eyes open for any likely candidates, even those coming up from junior high, but he'd never seen this boy before.

And he didn't see much now to impress him. Nice enough looking kid, all right. Rather deep-set gray eyes, close-cropped black hair, strong jaw. But there wasn't much heft to him. Five feet nine, 140 pounds, Jeffers guessed. At Westland High even the backs usually ranged from 155 to 180.

"Reporting kind of late, aren't you, son? We opened football workouts two weeks ago."

"Yes, sir, I know. I've just moved to town."

"I see." Again Jeffers measured the small, spare-built frame. "Had any experience?"

"One year at Mayville. Halfback."

"Uhuh." Jeffers was trying to recall something he'd heard about Mayville. Some little town about a hundred miles northwest. There was something he'd heard . . . he gave it up, he couldn't remember.

"You know, of course," he told the boy, "that as a transfer you won't be eligible this year."

The boy nodded. "I'm only a junior. Thought maybe I could work out with the squad. Keep in condition, learn the plays and all."

"Sure. It's the thing to do if you want to play next

year." Jeffers paused, smiling. "You know, son, you haven't told me your name yet."

"Clayburn. Scotty Clayburn."

Jeffers stiffened, the smile gone. *Now* he remembered. Mayville . . . Clayburn. How could he have forgotten!

And with the memory came the faint stir of an unwelcome suspicion. The coach framed the next question carefully. "You say your family has just moved to Westland?"

"My family didn't move here," the boy said. "I came by myself. That is, I'm going to be living with an uncle."

Jeffers sat very still a moment. Then he asked softly, "And your uncle's name, son?"

"John Durham."

The coach nodded. Now the whole picture was falling into place. And Lee Jeffers didn't like the looks of it.

The boy spoke, a little anxiously. "My moving here alone—that won't keep me from being eligible next year, will it?"

"Oh, no. You'll establish legal residence." Jeffers leaned forward. "Son, you gave up a whole year of eligibility to come down here. Mind if I ask you why?"

He watched closely for any reaction in the boy's face. There was none. The gray eyes met his without a flicker as the youth answered, "Westland High offers some courses I'm very interested in. Mayville didn't have them."

"I see," Jeffers said quietly. He wrote something on a slip of paper and handed it to the boy. "Take this to the equipment cage. Through that door and down the hall to your right."

When the boy had gone, Lee Jeffers sat there for a long while, his rugged features immobile. Then he stirred himself with a shrug and went back to checking his list. He had plenty of real problems to worry about. No use creating imaginary ones. At least, he *hoped* this would turn out to be only an imaginary one.

Both arms loaded with his newly issued equipment, Scotty Clayburn entered the dressing room. He stopped a moment, his gaze touched with wonder. He hadn't known they built dressing rooms this big and airy and full of sunlight. He looked down the long lines of lockers, glimpsed the gleaming tile of the showers at the far end of the room. It was certainly different from the dimly lighted, cramped quarters at Mayville.

A lot of things would be different here, of course. After all, this was one of the biggest high schools in the whole state of Texas. Almost three thousand students. More than the whole population of Mayville!

The state had larger towns than Westland. But where the bigger cities had several high schools, Westland, a town of some eighty thousand, clung to its one school. From what Scotty had heard, they were too proud of it to divide it.

Proud of their football teams, too. Year after year they turned out great teams, often contenders for the state's top Class AAAA championship. Westland was Big Time in schoolboy football. A long jump from little Class A Mayville.

Scotty walked over to the nearest boy—a big, brawny redhead who couldn't have been less than six feet three—and said, "Where would I find Locker 112?"

The red-haired giant looked down at Scotty and grinned in good-natured amusement. "Need a caddy to help you carry that stuff, don't you, pal?" He pointed. "Third row over, down near that end. Hope you make it."

"Thanks," Scotty said. He picked his way past half-clad boys, trying to shake off the lost feeling. A hundred or more boys in this room—and not a single familiar face. It was a strange sensation. Back in Mayville, every man on the squad was someone he'd known as far back as he could remember.

He found Locker 112 and dumped his gear. They'd given him good stuff, he noted. No worn-out hand-me-downs as he'd expected.

A voice grated in his ear. "You're in the wrong stall, aren't you, sonny boy? This is the A-Squad section."

Scotty looked around. The speaker, stripped to his shorts, had the size and build of a college back. Big shoulders, sleek and powerfully muscled legs. Only one thing marred his handsome blond features—a sort of faint sneer that lingered perpetually around his mouth.

"I wouldn't know," Scotty said mildly. "This is the locker the student manager assigned me."

"That jerk Rambo!" the handsome boy growled.

5

"He's always getting something fouled up. The B Squad dresses over in that far wing. You better go tell Rambo to change you."

Scotty smiled easily. "I guess he had some reason. This locker was empty and—"

"Rambo has to have a reason?" The big boy snorted. His voice became a harsh command. "Go on, tell him to give you a B-Squad locker."

Scotty's smile faded, but his voice was still soft. "How about you telling him. You're the one that seems worried about it. The locker suits me fine."

The blond face flushed red. "Smart, huh? Look, sonny—"

"Aw, knock it off, Cowan," the boy on Scotty's right spoke up. "How do you know the guy's not on the A Squad?"

"*Him!*" Cowan's voice was heavy with disdain. But he said no more for the moment, lapsing into a sulking silence. Then as he stood up to leave, he said, "You won't be back here tomorrow. I'll see that Rambo puts his B-Squad boys where they belong."

Scotty, pulling on socks, didn't bother to look up.

"Don't let Cowan worry you," the boy on the right said. "Sometimes he gets to thinking he owns the place."

"Is it against the rules," Scotty asked, "for the B and A squads to locker together?"

"No, really doesn't matter. We just group the squads for convenience. Cowan just likes to throw his weight around. Acts right childish at times. Heck of a good fullback though."

"Looks like he could handle the job," Scotty observed.

"Yeh. Big and fast. . . . Say, haven't I seen you before? Yeh . . . this morning. We're in the same home room." The boy held out a hand. "I'm Dave Franklin."

"Scotty Clayburn." Scotty took the hand. "But I wouldn't remember who I saw in home room." He grinned. "I was too dizzy trying to figure out all that enrollment detail."

"Throw the red tape at you, don't they," the other agreed. He was not so big as Cowan, but big enough, his 175 pounds nicely proportioned over a six-foot frame. His face broke into a grin. "That was pretty good, the way you let Cowan rave on—you knowing all the time you were on the A Squad."

"But I didn't know," Scotty said. "Nobody told me."

"Well, I can tell you. I know you're a junior. All our home room are juniors. And they don't let juniors play on the B Squad, only sophomores. Juniors have to make the A Squad, or they're out. You're a transfer, aren't you?"

Scotty nodded.

"That's tough. Having to lay out a year, I mean. Your folks just moved in, I guess, or you'd have reported sooner."

"My folks didn't move to Westland. Just me."

Dave Franklin waited for more information, but none came. He frowned, puzzled. Why would a guy want to change schools if he didn't have to—lose a whole year of football? Well, that was Clayburn's business, he guessed. And Clayburn sure wasn't offering to explain.

Dave said, "You might like to know this. Coach will start cutting the squad next week. He'll trim the A Squad to a little under fifty men. It may be a little tough, Scotty, your getting started late. And you're—" He broke off.

He'd been about to say, "You're pretty small and light for this team," Scotty knew.

"What I mean," Dave resumed, "your getting in late might— Well, anything I can help you with, let me know. Even if you can't play this year, you don't want to get cut off the squad."

"Sure don't," Scotty said. "And thanks. I'll probably need all the help I can get."

Still curious, Dave said, "Bet you've played plenty of football though. I can tell the way you got into those pads."

"Yeh." Scotty pulled on his jersey. "I've played some."

Dave waited. But the new boy said no more.

Funny sort of guy, Dave thought. Nice kid, but mighty close-mouthed. The way he clammed up about himself, you'd almost think he was trying to hide something.

8

Chapter Two

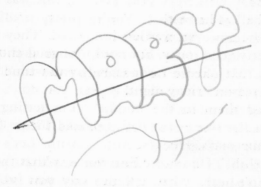

Tall and rangy Ceph Hodges, Westland's quarterback, took the ball from center, pivoted, and shoved the leather toward Hal Leighton, the right half. Leighton, slanting left, barreled into the line, running low and hard.

Leighton, however, didn't have the ball. Hodges had moved on, slipping it to Cowan as the fullback came by. Defensive end, tackle, and backer were split apart by well-timed blocks, and Cowan hit the opening. He pulled wide, cut back to escape one tackler, and ran another ten yards before two men wrestled him down.

Pretty football, Scotty Clayburn was thinking. For half an hour he'd watched the scrimmage, and he could see why Westland teams lost very few ball games. The precision of Coach Jeffers' T stuff, even this early in the year, was beautiful to see. The linemen were big, but they weren't carrying any lard around. They were quick-moving boys who hit fast and made leather pop. Timing was exact. The backs, fakers and all, ran hard, and they were very fast. Yes, sir, this was high school football at its best.

Lee Jeffers, however, was less impressed. They were looking pretty good today, but not quite good enough. He wanted that offense razor-sharp by the time they opened the season Friday night.

He joined them in the huddle. "I'm letting this unit stay in the rest of the day," he told them. "Run through your plays, Hodges. Mix 'em up. Let's look like a ball club!" He lowered his voice so that the defense couldn't hear. "First, I want to see that fullback counter. It's been a little ragged. Hodges, don't let Cowan have to wait for that ball. Leighton, make like you've really got that thing. Keegan, I want to see that backer taken out this time— I mean *out*. Okay, men, make it go!"

Hodges faked to Leighton, gave it to Cowan. The fullback plunged to the left of the middle guard in the five-man defensive line. A great hole yawned in front of him. Middle guard two-teamed. Tackle cross-blocked. Backer wheeled away by the fast-charging Del Keegan, coming across from left tackle. Cowan had plenty of running room.

The big fullback made good use of it. He slapped

10

down a halfback, veered to the right, and outran the safety man with powerful, ground-eating strides. Jeffers blew the whistle, but Cowan galloped on another twenty yards before he halted the run.

Jeffers said, "That was better. Much better. And, Cowan, watch the whistle. You'll get all the running you want before this is over."

The coach meant it, literally. Rex Cowan, called up from the B team as a sophomore last year, had proved quite a sensation in the late-season games. The fame had gone to his head a bit, but Jeffers figured he could handle that. Cowan was his strongest ball carrier, and he meant to build a lot of his running game around the big boy.

As the scrimmage went on, Cowan was called often, carrying on slants, power plays, traps. And he was really going. His mates were clearing him past the line; more often than not he was breaking clear. And when the downfield blocks didn't arrive, he was simply running around or over the halfbacks and safety.

On defense, third and fourth stringers were shuttling in and out. Off to one side stood a group of nondescript stragglers, bottom-of-the-barrel boys who hadn't seen any action yet. With this group was Scotty Clayburn.

Scotty had taken only a limited part in the day's workout—calisthenics, hitting the dummy, some hand-off practice in which Eck Foster, the backfield coach, had teamed him with a fifth- or sixth-string combination.

He watched now as another play took form. Cowan was carrying inside tackle, then pivoting away from the backer, running wide. The halfback caught a piece of Cowan's leg. The big ball carrier jerked his leg with a snap, and he was loose, and gone again.

Jim Boone, the line coach, who was working with the defense, grumbled in mild disgust. He turned to the group of stragglers. "We got any backs around here that know how to tackle?"

The scrubs were silent. They knew Boone didn't expect them to answer. He might send somebody in; more likely he wouldn't. Mainly, it was just his way of letting off steam.

But Scotty Clayburn figured the man was asking a question. So he answered. He raised his hand high.

Behind him, someone snickered softly.

Boone was giving him a narrow-eyed appraisal, noting the spare frame, the skinny shanks. "Okay. . . . Wait. This is your first day out, sonny. You ready for this?"

Scotty was already pulling on the red half-jersey that identified the defense. "Yes, sir. I think so."

"You better *know* so," Boone said, not urgently. "Okay, get in there at right half." He muttered to himself, "At that, he couldn't be any worse than what I've had in there."

It was the second play after that. They sprung Cowan on the counter, with a cutback to the right. The fullback came roaring through the line. His churning knees tore him away from one tackler. His straight-arm eliminated another. Big Red McGraw, the right end, arrived on schedule, wiping out the safety man. Cowan thundered past, cutting for the sideline.

Then something like a leaping panther flashed across his path. One instant Cowan was loose; the next he was flat on his face, his legs pinned together.

Scotty Clayburn bounced up and returned to his position. Cowan got up slowly. Too astonished for anger, he said, "Where'd *he* come from?"

"A good question," murmured Red McGraw. He was peering at the slender figure with interest. Wasn't that the kid who'd been looking for Locker 112?

Jim Boone was looking too, a wisp of a smile at the corners of his mouth. He was thinking: *Wow! Have we got something here? Or was that just a fluke? We'll just watch and see.*

Three plays later they ran the counter again, with Cowan cutting left this time. Dick Allred, a rock-hard 160-pounder at left half, swung in front to block out the right half. Scotty waited, measuring the exact instant when Allred would make contact. Just before that instant arrived, Scotty made a quick feint to his left. Allred hurled a block. Scotty skipped back to his left. Allred's heavy hip brushed his leg as he sprang for Cowan. Scotty's shoulder made contact and his arms snapped shut. Cowan spun half around and fell.

This time, anger burned in Cowan's face. He snarled at Allred, "You call that blocking! You turned him into me!"

Allred said dourly, "I didn't turn him anywhere, pal. He suckered me."

"That guy!" Cowan snorted. "I wouldn't admit it."

13

"And that's not all," Allred added. "I've got a hunch that little joker's going to be hard for anybody to block."

Cowan laughed. "Wait till I get a shot at him. I'll show you how it's done."

In the huddle Allred said, "Cowan wants to show me how to block that right half. Let's give him a chance, Ceph."

The quarterback shot them a look, then shrugged. "Okay. Make it forty-eight. Take him off, Cowan."

"I'll rattle his teeth," Cowan growled.

They unraveled the play, a crisscross. Allred and Leighton, the halfbacks, crossed paths and Cowan powered ahead. From Ceph Hodges' motions, he could have fed it to any one of them. Scotty, seeing Leighton coming wide, arms cuddled, started to move in.

Then in that split second, instinct warned him. His eye gave proof of the warning—the left end and tackle weren't blocking; they were going through. That meant downfield blocking to the opposite side. The play was going the other way!

Scotty started across field. From the corner of his eye he glimpsed Cowan, bearing down with vicious intent. Scotty did not feint or dodge. He simply turned on a burst of sheer speed. Cowan lunged desperately—and missed.

The safety man was chasing Allred, pinning him to the sideline. Allred cut back. Scotty hit him, rolling him down.

"Nice work, Cowan," Allred said as they huddled. "You really took him off. You really rattled his teeth."

14

Cowan, cheeks flaming, growled, "He was playing out of position."

Red McGraw drawled, "Awful inconsiderate of him —not to stand still so you could hit him."

"Cut it," Hodges said. "Coach will be in here wanting to know what goes."

Leighton spoke up. "That scrub is pretty good, but he's trying to cover too much ground. Let's give him old forty-six-R."

They ran it. Hodges hid the ball neatly, and the faking was good. Scotty moved in warily. The left end's block on the tackle tabbed it as a running play, not a pass. But where was the ball?

Then he saw Cowan and Hodges emerge around right end, Allred right behind them in a crouching run, arms folded to his midriff. Scotty hurried over.

But Allred didn't have the ball. Leighton had it, going left, cutting inside end, bursting into open ground Scotty had vacated. Too late, Scotty saw it. He tried to turn back. A bone-jarring block slammed him to the turf. Leighton raced on, unhampered. Jeffers blew the whistle.

Chuck Beddo, the 200-pound tackle who'd thrown the block, grinned. "That, scrub, is our special for eager-beaver halfbacks. Known as the reverse."

Scotty wasn't listening. He was thinking back. The end had been blocking the tackle *in*, not out. He should have known the play was coming his way.

And Jim Boone was thinking: *He looked bad on that one. But I'd lay a bet he won't make that same mistake again.*

15

In the huddle Hodges said, "Now the sixty-F pass. We'll make a believer out of that guy."

They lined up with Leighton a flanker on the right. The end came straight down, and Scotty picked him up. He also saw Allred swinging out wide. The backer wasn't covering Allred. Nobody was on Allred. But Scotty had left his assigned territory once, and he wasn't doing it again. He stayed with the deep man, the end—until Hodges threw. Then, the instant the ball took flight, he let the end go and sprinted.

There was some luck in it. Hodges, holding the ball a split second too long, passed just a fraction short. Allred braked, took one step back, and jumped. Out of nowhere came a soaring figure, obscuring his vision of the ball. Hands closed on the leather, snaking it away.

Scotty was running when his feet hit the ground. He heard Allred hit the turf in a futile tackle as he streaked for the sideline. Cowan was coming fast to cut him off. Behind raced Hodges, protecting the inside. Others streamed in Hodges' wake.

Scotty measured the narrowing slit at the sideline and knew he couldn't make it. He slowed his pace a fraction. And Cowan made his move—a murderous block aimed for Scotty's thighs. It was perfectly timed to hammer him out of bounds.

Except that Scotty was no longer running. He was standing still for one frozen instant, cleats grinding turf in a shuddering stop. Cowan's bulk went hurtling past and hit the sod. Scotty feinted a shoulder at Hodges, then sprang back for the sideline. An explosive burst of speed pulled him away from Hodges' clawing hands. He was sprinting free over the goal line when he heard the long blast of Jeffers' whistle.

The coach was calling them in. "Two laps around the field and go in. That's all for today."

Scotty handed the coach the ball. Jeffers looked at him intently for a moment, then said, "Skip the laps, son. Take a shower. For a first day, you've had your exercise."

Jim Boone loomed in front of Jeffers, grinning. "How you like my new right half?" the line coach said. "I've been holding him out—a secret weapon."

Eck Foster joined them. The backfield coach gave Jeffers a sober look. "It hit me all at once. You know who that kid is?"

"Name is Clayburn," Jeffers said.

"Yeh? Jog your memory, Lee. That's *the* Clayburn. The kid who was such a sensation up at Mayville last year. Written up in papers all over the state, even if he was only in Class A. Scored forty-three touchdowns, about half of them on long runs. Missed about three points-after the whole season. Had something like three out of four average on pass completions. Remember now?"

Jeffers smiled wanly. "Really a hound for statistics, aren't you, Eck?"

"Well . . . did you remember? Did you know who that kid was when he came out today?"

"Yes," Jeffers said quietly. "Yes . . . I knew."

And he wasn't sure he was happy about it. Not at all sure.

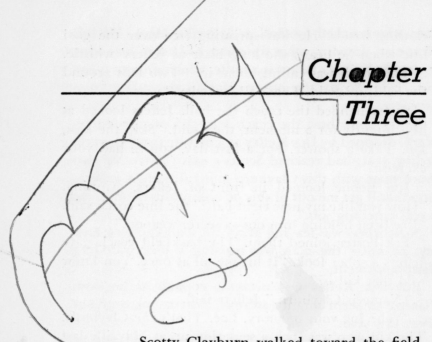

Chapter Three

Scotty Clayburn walked toward the field-house, feeling mixed emotions. The taste of scrimmage had made him realize how much he was going to miss playing football this year—actually playing.

Practice was all right, but it could never match the real thing. If he were back in Mayville now, he'd be looking forward to the opening game this Friday. Here in Westland, he'd have to wait a whole year for that thrill.

Thoughts of Mayville disturbed him for another reason too. It wasn't the homesickness; he could learn to overcome that. It was something else—a memory. A memory not at all pleasant. . . .

He was in the office of Doc Kelley, the big, red-faced

18

man who coached football at Mayville High. He felt ill at ease, dreading what the coach had asked him here to do. On Kelley's face was a smile, which did not quite hide from Scotty the bitter glint in the man's pale-blue eyes.

Scotty knew how the coach felt. An unguarded remark, dropped by Doc Kelley at a private party the preceding year, had reached Scotty's ears: "Give me two more years with this Clayburn and I'll build a reputation that'll get me out of this one-horse dump and into a real coaching job."

Now Scotty was leaving Mayville. And knowing Kelley, he knew the man was nursing a sour, rankling disappointment.

But Doc Kelley was pleasant enough as he said, "Going to seem mighty strange, not having you out there this year."

"I'm going to miss it too, Coach," Scotty said, and he meant it. It had been a hard decision—leaving his home, his school, his lifelong friends—going away to spend his last two years of high school in a big, strange town.

"Frankly," Kelley said, "I don't know who I'll get to take your place."

Scotty felt uncomfortable. "You'll get somebody, Coach. You've got some good boys back this year."

A little rancor crept into Doc Kelley's voice. "I don't have anybody who can roll up fifteen hundred yards rushing. Probably never will have again."

"It was a good club last year," Scotty said. "I had a lot of help." He wanted to add "and a mighty good coach." It would be the polite thing to say. But Scotty could never bring himself to say a thing he didn't believe, even for the sake of politeness.

Actually, he didn't think much of Kelley's coaching, though he'd always kept that opinion strictly to himself. Most of Mayville's success last season, Scotty thought, had been due to Kelley's one assistant, Johnny Alderson. Alderson was a fine instructor in fundamentals, and his calm, encouraging manner had inspired the boys a lot of times when Kelley's bluster threatened to upset and confuse them.

But the thing Scotty liked least about Kelley was something else—the man's tendency to encourage dirty play. He had ways of putting it, of course, to cover up. He'd say, "This Number Fourteen on their club is smart and fancy and he'll beat you if you don't watch out. But something tells me a few good hard jolts will slow him down. When you tackle him, tackle him for keeps. Nothing dirty, you understand. . . ."

The boys knew what he really meant, though, and those who were inclined to dirty play had their cue and encouragement. Despite this, most of the Mayville kids played it clean; but there'd been a few who didn't. Scotty was thinking of two of them—a linebacker and a tackle—who had done their best to "get" a triple-threat star in the district play-off last year. The boy had stayed in till late in the game anyway, playing a key part in Mayville's defeat; but when he'd finally gone out, he'd carried with him a twisted knee, not to mention a bloody face, barked shins, and assorted bruises. To Scotty, it had left a taste even more bitter than the loss of the game.

Maybe that had made it a little easier for him to leave Mayville—and Doc Kelley.

Kelley was saying, "You sprung this on us real sudden. I only heard about it yesterday." The big man's eyes narrowed. "There's rumors of this and that, Scotty. What's the straight of it, kid? Why're you leaving Mayville?"

"It's just this, Coach," Scotty said. "When I finish high school, I want to start helping Mom support the family."

He didn't have to explain why it was so important to help. Doc Kelley knew all about that. Knew about the oil-tank explosion that had taken his father's life a year ago and had left his mother with four children to support. There hadn't been much insurance, and few job opportunities for her in Mayville. Besides, the small children—Scotty was the oldest—needed her at home and she couldn't very well leave them during the day. She had managed somehow with a little dress-making business, but it hadn't been easy.

"To be a real help to Mom," Scotty went on, "I'll need a good job that pays well. There's not much in Mayville, and—well, for a long time I've been interested in radio and TV. I'd like to be an expert repairman, maybe a technician someday. Mr. Hillyard says I sort of have a talent for that stuff." Mr. Hillyard was the general-science teacher.

"That's where Westland comes in," Scotty ex-

21

plained. "They have vocational courses in radio and television. I'll be prepared for a job as soon as I graduate. Then, living in a bigger town like that, I'll have a better chance for job contacts."

"Well," Kelley said, "I hope it works out." His tone implied he didn't think it would. "I just hate to see you lose a whole year of football, sweet player like you."

"I hate to lose that year too," Scotty said. "But much as I like football, I figure training for the job comes first."

Doc sighed. "I don't suppose there's anything we can do to change your mind."

Scotty shook his head. "Mom and I have talked it over a lot. We feel it's the best thing."

Doc leaned forward. "You know, you've got friends in Mayville that'd like to help—to keep you here."

Scotty looked puzzled. "I don't get you, Coach."

"Your mother has been up against it." Doc's tone was sympathetic. "I know fellows in town who'd likely be glad to advance her some money. We might call it a loan—"

"Mom wouldn't consider it," Scotty interrupted with quiet emphasis. "We don't want that kind of help."

Doc smiled tightly. "Well, now, Scotty, I was just wondering if someone down at Westland hadn't done something like that—say, offered you a little inducement?"

"No, sir!" Scotty felt a touch of anger.

"No offense meant, son," Doc said placatingly. "It

has been done, you know. But I'll take your word for it—nothing like that in your case." He got up. "We better get into the dressing room. Boys should be about ready to take the field."

"Just a minute, Coach." Scotty hadn't liked this idea much from the start; now he liked it even less. "I think I'd better lay off the speech-making."

Kelley looked at him. "You're leaving on a bus for Westland in an hour. How many of the boys have you seen since you decided to leave Mayville?"

"Well . . . only two or three."

Doc waved a hand. "There you are. You wouldn't want to go off without seeing the others. Here's your chance, while they're all together."

"Sure, I want to see them. But this speech—"

"You don't have to make it an oration, kid. Just tell the boys good-by and good luck—any little thing you want to say. They'll appreciate it."

In the locker room some thirty boys were in the last stages of donning football gear. There were the usual sounds—loud talk, banging locker doors, cleats on concrete.

"Attention, everybody!" Doc Kelley boomed.

The noise subsided. Cleats scuffed the floor as the boys moved into a loosely gathered group. Then silence.

Doc put an arm on Scotty's shoulder. "I don't have to introduce this guy. As most of you know, he won't be back with us this year. He wants to say a few farewell words to his old team buddies before he leaves."

Scotty stood there, his mouth dry, his knees suddenly

weak. The moment he'd dreaded was here, but some-how it was much worse than he'd imagined. It wasn't just the embarrassment of "making a speech." There was something deeper—a kind of panic. Maybe it was the stony silence. Or the cold, unblinking stares.

He heard his voice, coming as from a great distance. "I guess you heard I'm leaving Mayville to attend Westland High. Some of you I haven't seen, so I wanted to say . . . I sure hate to leave. It was really great, playing football with you guys . . . I can't tell you how much I'll miss—"

His voice choked to a stop. Something here was all wrong. Were these the same boys he'd known all these years—his old friends, teammates? These were the faces of strangers—cold, hostile.

He was speaking again. "I sure hope you have a great season . . . I'll be wishing you a lot of luck."

After that it was a hazy, nightmarish memory, with only a few sharp details piercing through the haze. Only two boys stepped out to shake his hand: "Hate to see you go, Scotty. Good luck." "Yeh, same here, Scotty." . . . The others hung back. They addressed each other, not him. "Too good for Mayville" . . . "Can't blame a guy for taking a better thing, I guess" . . . "Must be nice to have a rich uncle" . . . "Wonder how much allowance he's getting to play for *them*."

Then Kelley's hoarse voice broke in. "Scotty's got to catch a bus, so he'll be running along." Then softly, "Sorry, kid. Some of the boys are awfully disappointed, I guess. Had no idea they'd take it that way."

But Kelley had known. He'd known all the time.

He'd planned it that way. Probably had planted the idea in their minds. And Scotty could almost hear Kelley, after he'd gone, using it to fire them up with a big pep talk: "Okay, so you lost your star. He walked out and left you cold. So what are you going to do about it? Give up? Tuck your tails like a bunch of whipped dogs? Or will you get in there and fight harder? . . ."

It still seemed unreal—that memory. Like an impossible thing that couldn't have happened. But it *had* happened. Friends of many years were friends no longer. The anger and bitterness would cool in time, of course. Most of them would later be ashamed of what they'd said. But they would never be quite the same friends again. They'd never quite understand why he had to go to Westland. They'd remember him as the guy who walked out on his old team and went after something better for himself.

So he had to start all over again, here at Westland. Had to make new friends.

And he could do that here. Westland was a big place. He was just one new face among hundreds of new faces. The fact that he was a transfer who had played football elsewhere would create no more than a ripple. Here, he could go his way quietly and find new friendships.

It was something to look forward to.

25

Chapter
Four

The Westland players did not know yet what the coaches knew. Later some of them would remember reading in the papers the year before about a back up there in some little town who was rewriting the record book. Now, however, they knew only one thing—that this new fellow with the featherweight build and the quiet manner was a football player. They were convinced of that.

All except Rex Cowan.

As a group of them trudged in from the field, the big fullback was saying, "So he looks good on a few plays—going in there fresh when the rest of us were fagged at the end of a long workout. What does that prove?"

"Be your age, Cowan," Red McGraw said. "There's not one back in a thousand can really pull off that stunt he pulled on you and Hodges. The guy is good." Then the tall end added, "What I can't figure, where has he been all this time?"

Dave Franklin spoke up. "He's a transfer."

"Naturally," Dick Allred said. "But from where?"

"He didn't say. In fact he didn't say much of anything."

"You know," McGraw mused, "I'm beginning to smell a rodent in the pantry."

"What do you mean?" Cowan frowned.

"I mean this fellow blowing in here so mysterious-like reminds me of a fairy tale I once heard, chums. It seems that once upon a time in the old days here at Westland—"

"You're off base, Red," Franklin broke in. "I've heard that tale too, and I say—well, this kid just isn't the type."

"You're a nice guy, Dave," McGraw said. "You trust people too easily."

"Would you smart clucks mind telling us what you're talking about?" Cowan asked.

"Forget it," Red replied. "If it's bad news, you'll hear it soon enough. If not, we'd better drop the subject."

"Anyway," Allred said, "he can't play till next year—which might be lucky for me."

"It's no help to me," Franklin said. "Next year is when I'm hoping to break into that starting backfield."

"Me, I'm waiting to see," Cowan said. "I've got a

hunch our little fancy Dan will fade when the grind gets tough."

McGraw chuckled. "He sure faded today—when you and Hodges boxed him at the sideline. Must have faded out of sight."

"Funnyman McGraw!" Cowan growled.

They were at their lockers when Scotty Clayburn came back from the shower. Dave Franklin greeted him with a frown of mock indignation. "Okay for you —letting me worry about your making the squad. From now on I'll do all my worrying about old Dave." He grinned. "I guess you got a laugh out of it, at that— my thinking *you'd* need help."

"Not at all, Dave," Scotty said. "I've got a lot to learn—that T formation, for instance."

"That T wasn't much of a mystery to you out there today."

"That was defense. I've had to play against it lots of times. But running it on offense will be something else. We had spins and handoffs in our single wing, but nothing like this T stuff. Everything happens so quick!"

"Single-wing man, eh? Where did you play?"

"Tailback."

"I mean *where*—what school?"

"Oh . . . Mayville."

It didn't mean anything to Dave. He didn't remember the preceding year's newspaper stories.

He was studying the slender boy, seeing some things he'd failed to notice before. The new boy was small and light, yes. But now Dave also noted that extra width to the shoulders; the hard ridges of muscle on back and chest; the telltale bulge behind and just above the knees—the muscle that gives a running back that explosive burst of speed when he needs it.

Dave raised his voice. "Anyway, I think we can let you stay in the A-Squad section. How about it, Rex?"

Cowan turned, sneering. "Too bad, Franklin, you can't play football like you can wisecrack." He left for the shower.

Dave Franklin flushed, struck at a sensitive spot. He was the biggest back on the squad, except for Cowan, but had faint prospect of making the first team. All through junior high and his B-Squad year, Dave had been nudged off the lineup by smaller men. It wasn't nice to be reminded of it.

"Guess I shouldn't have needled him," Dave said. "No use giving him something else to hold against you."

"There's no reason for me and Cowan to have trouble," Scotty said quietly. "Let's forget it."

"You've got the right idea. Trouble is, you made him look bad today. And he's awfully slow to forget."

A small youth with curly black hair came up, saying in a startling bass voice, "Clayburn, Mr. Jeffers wants to see you in his office when you're dressed." Then he was gone, hurrying. Chigger Rambo, the student manager, thwarted by nature from being an athlete, was proud of his job and took it very seriously. He always seemed to be in a hurry.

"Now you get the book of plays," Dave told Scotty.

But it was more than that, Scotty learned, when he reported to the head coach a few minutes later.

Jeffers looked up. "Close the door and have a seat, son. Want to talk with you a few minutes."

A tiny warning bell rang in Scotty's mind, despite the coach's casual and friendly manner.

"How old are you, Scotty?"

"Sixteen. Be seventeen in November."

"Weigh about one forty?"

Scotty began to feel a little more relaxed. "One forty-six, sir. Ten pounds more than last season."

Jeffers thought: It figures. A little heavier than he looks . . . small but tough and wiry . . . type that grows slowly and develops coordination early . . . already has the swift, controlled reflexes of a twenty-year-old . . . but he'll never put on a lot of pounds.

The coach said, "You showed a good deal of finesse out there today for a sixteen-year-old. Your old Mayville coach—Kelley, I believe, is his name—must have been a good tutor."

"Yes, sir," Scotty said. "Another man, a friend of mine, helped me a lot too."

He let it go at that. Actually, he'd learned very little from Kelley. It had been Bill Mabry who'd taught him everything—Bill Mabry, who'd been holding the fire hose along with Scotty's father that day the oil tank exploded and killed four men.

It had all begun one day when Bill, a former college player, had stopped to watch some youngsters, Scotty

30

among them, scrimmaging on a vacant lot. Bill had called Scotty aside and said, "Kid, you're a runt, but you've got something. You want to learn to be a *real* football player?"

That had been the beginning. For three years Bill Mabry spent endless hours with Scotty out in the Clayburn's big backyard or in the vacant lot, teaching him how to handle the ball, how to pass and kick it, how to block and tackle; drilling him on such fine points as the straight-arm, pivot, sidestep. By the time Scotty entered high school, he was master of the fundamentals, needing only game experience. He got plenty of that as a 125-pound freshman, playing almost half the time as understudy tailback. "You're on your way now, kid," Bill had said. "Next year you'll be a star."

Next year. That had been last year—the football season neither Bill nor Scotty's dad had lived to see. . . .

Jeffers was saying, "You told me you came to Westland to get some courses your old school didn't offer. What courses, exactly? And why is it so important to you to have them?"

"Radio and television," Scotty said. "I'm hoping they'll help me get a good job."

"You're planning to go right to work? No college?"

"That's right, sir. I couldn't even think about college. You see"—Scotty paused uncertainly—"I'm afraid I'd have to go into a lot of detail to explain that."

Jeffers said quietly, "I'd like to have the details, Scotty. All the details—if you don't mind."

As briefly as he could, Scotty gave him the whole

story—his father's death, the need for helping his mother, his idea of training himself here for the work he'd like to follow.

When Scotty finished, Jeffers nodded slowly. Then he said, "One more question. How did you find out about these courses at Westland?"

Scotty thought a moment. "Why—from Uncle John. For a year Uncle John has been trying to get me to come down and live with him and Aunt Alice—they don't have any children. Then he found out I was interested in that kind of work, and he told me about the courses here."

"So you decided to take him up on it. And football had nothing to do with your transfer. Right?"

"You mean . . . Oh, you mean did I come here mainly to play football. No, sir. If I'd been thinking mostly of football, I'd have stayed at Mayville—and not lose a whole season."

Jeffers leaned over the desk, his eyes a little grim. "You know, Scotty, I believe you. But I'm afraid a lot of people are not going to believe you."

Scotty flushed. "I don't quite get that, sir."

Jeffers took a deep breath. "We've got a little problem, Scotty, you and I. Once today I thought I'd ignore it, but I've changed my mind. It won't be ignored. I've decided you deserve to know—to face it with your eyes open." He paused. "What I have to say is strictly between you and me."

"Sure, I understand," Scotty said. So his premonition of trouble had been right after all.

"Some years back," Jeffers said, "some of the larger

schools in the state made a practice of raiding little schools for prize football players. They'd spot a fine player in some small school, especially some boy whose folks were hard up, and the first thing you know this kid's dad would be moving his family to the big town, holding down a nice job—a job nobody would have thought of offering him if his son hadn't been a star football player. You follow me?"

"Yes, sir. I suppose the transfer rule has stopped all that now."

"Not entirely. Even now a few schools are willing to go for a boy and keep him two years for one year's play. Understand, the school itself doesn't do this. It's done by certain men in the community who fancy themselves staunch supporters of the school's athletics. Of course, their idea of good athletics is winning all the games."

Jeffers stopped, fingering a scratch pad on his desk. Scotty, troubled by a sense of foreboding, said nothing.

The coach looked up. "Now here's the bad part, Scotty. At one time Westland was one of the worst offenders in the state at this recruiting business. One Westland state champion team had four key players they'd lured from small towns. We got quite a reputation—not a nice reputation—for raiding little towns for football players. I say 'we.' I wasn't coaching here then. Nor was the present administration in office. For several years now we've been extra alert, trying to keep our skirts clean and live down the bad name we got. It hasn't always been easy. It's a football town, Scotty, pretty rabid about winning. We still have some 'supporters' who'd like to bring in outside talent at times. So far, we've been able to forestall them. In fact, I've made it pretty plain I simply would not use a boy brought here in that manner."

Scotty felt a sudden fear. "You mean you won't use anyone who's transferred?"

"Not that, Scotty. Sure, we have an occasional transfer. People do move in, naturally. But the circumstances have always been above suspicion—and it so happened none of the boys who moved in were outstanding players. . . . And that's what makes *your* case different—and a problem."

Scotty sat rigidly still. He was beginning to see a little of what was coming.

"You see, Scotty, if you were just another ball player, it wouldn't matter. The public would hardly know you were here. But we might as well face the facts—you were no ordinary ball player at Mayville. You were publicized all over the state. And now, all at once, you transfer to Westland. You move here by yourself, while your mother and family still live in Mayville. You can see what some people are likely to think."

Scotty could see now. And he felt a touch of bitterness. Back in Mayville he'd been unjustly accused. Must he face the same unjust suspicion here too?

One thing was very plain now. He'd been pretty foolish to think he could just drop quietly into the life of this school, unknown and unnoticed.

Finally he spoke, the words choking in his throat.

34

"I don't want to hurt the school or the team. If you want me to turn in my suit—"

"You'll get to know me better than that, Scotty," Jeffers said. "No, we don't solve problems by running away from them. You and I must understand each other and work together."

Scotty swallowed. "Yes, sir. If there's any way I can help—"

"You can help a great deal. The main thing is to be forewarned. First, there are the newspapers. We have two papers here. The sportswriter for one of them, the *Times*, prints the truth and plays fair with coaches, players, and readers. Unfortunately, the other one does not. His name is Spinks Pinley, and he writes for the *Express*. He may try to dig up evidence that we recruited you away from Mayville. Not finding any, he may manufacture some out of his own imagination. If he interviews you, be careful what you say! He's tricky. He'll put words in your mouth if he can. Get what I mean?"

Scotty nodded.

"Then there's another thing. If talk gets started around town or inside the school, ignore it. Just keep a closed mouth and let the talk wear itself out." The coach got up and grasped Scotty's hand. "I'm counting on you, son. Maybe nothing much will happen. We'll hope so. But it's better to be on guard."

Scotty returned the grip. "I understand, sir. And thanks a lot."

"Oh . . . I almost forgot. Come by here before your

first class tomorrow. Coach Foster will give you the plays and explain about keeping a notebook."

"Yes, sir. I'll be here."

Outside, dusk had fallen. All the other players had left. Scotty hurried past the huge, sprawling layout of coral-red brick buildings that was Westland High—the music building, the shop wing, and on to the curb in front of the main building where his uncle had said he would wait.

Uncle John was there, lounging behind the wheel of the Cadillac. His voice boomed, "Get in here, boy. They kept you long enough. Coach have you on a board of strategy or something?"

Scotty avoided direct reply. "Sorry you had to wait. You should let me ride the bus."

The Cadillac leaped ahead. "Later," his uncle said. "After you learn the streets and can find your way home."

Middle-aged John Durham was a large, hearty man, loud-voiced and likable. And he was wealthy. Just how wealthy Scotty didn't know. But he did know it hadn't always been so. There'd been times, some years ago, when his dad had "loaned" his uncle money for a supply of groceries or the week's rent. That had been before one of Uncle John's oil-lease gambles had finally paid off—and had started him on the way to a fortune-making oil business.

"How'd it go today?" Uncle John asked. "You get in on the workout?"

"I got in a little," Scotty said.

"You'll be getting in plenty before long. Jeffers will

be grooming you for next year. What do you think of the coach?"

Scotty was surprised at the question. "He's tops. From what I've seen, I'd say one of the finest—"

"Good man, all right," his uncle broke in. "Nice fellow too. Hope he has a good season. Like to see him here next year."

"You mean he's thinking of leaving?"

John Durham chuckled. "You don't know Westland, kid. I mean he'll have to go to at least the semifinal this year or his contract won't be renewed. He hasn't put a team in the state finals in three years. Eliminated in the quarter-final once, beat out in the district last two years."

Scotty found it hard to believe. "You mean a coach loses three games in three years, and he's in danger of getting fired!"

"It's a football town, son. A football-*crazy* town, I guess you'd say. They're used to winning and they don't like to lose. They want that state title again, and they think we've got the boys to win it. But I'm not worrying. We'll win it next year—with you in there. You are going to make us a sweet little football player, Scotty. You'll be the hottest thing to hit this town in a long time."

Quietly, Scotty said, "Uncle John, I haven't even made the team yet. And I wish you'd promise not to talk about it to other folks."

His uncle laughed heartily. "You can be modest, Scotty—but not me. I'm proud of you. You're going to be quite a personage around Westland. Reporters will be interviewing you, running stories about our bright hope for next year. You're going to be in the spotlight. Might as well get used to it."

Scotty fell silent. The "spotlight" was the one thing he did *not* want. All he wanted was a chance to get some education and play some football because he loved the game. But he was afraid people weren't going to let it be that simple.

Already he was beginning to see it. Avoiding the dangers Jeffers had warned him about wasn't going to be easy.

Chapter Five

Alice Durham said, "He certainly didn't eat much. You suppose the boy is worried about something?"

She and her husband were seated at the dinner table. Scotty had just excused himself and gone to his room.

John Durham shrugged. "Things are a little strange yet to him. Give him time to get adjusted. And don't worry about his eating. He'll be putting away two-inch sirloins before long."

Alice Durham, a slender and attractive woman who looked younger than her forty years, mused, "He's such a nice boy. I wish his mother would let us do more for him. We could buy him a little car, some nice clothes. It would be fun—like having a son of our own."

Her husband shook his head. "You know how proud that sister of mine is. I had enough trouble talking her out of paying his board. Had to remind her of the times she and Charlie helped me in the old days. . . . No, Alice, we'll have to do it their way. Scotty made pretty good money at the supermarket in the summer. Saved enough to take care of his clothes and incidentals. He'll feel happier buying his own."

Alice Durham was thoughtful. "When you think about it, John, none of our close friends has any children his age—for us to introduce him to, I mean. I wonder if he'll get lonely here."

"Alice, you're a worrier. He'll meet plenty of young folks at school. Don't fret yourself about that kid. He'll be the most popular boy in Westland High."

At that moment Scotty did feel somewhat lonely. The house—a rambling ranch style, located on a large wooded lot in one of the town's exclusive additions— was so big and quiet. And sort of empty. His room, with its luxurious furnishings, somehow seemed cold and unfriendly.

Then he felt ashamed at the thought. This was to be his home a long time, and he must learn to like it —and to appreciate it. His uncle and aunt were trying to make everything nice for him, and he should be grateful. Aunt Alice was really swell. Pretty too, though not as pretty as his mother.

Which reminded him. He must write his mother a letter.

He wrote about the first day at school. He was enrolled in English, American History, Geometry, and

Radio. They had a wonderful laboratory in electricity and electronics. Next year he would be able to take Advanced Electronics. Everybody had been swell to him, and he was going to study hard.

He told her about the football setup. Coach Jeffers was a fine man and really knew his stuff. They had a lot of fine material here, but he thought he could make the team next year.

He said hello to the smaller kids—eight-year-old Ann and Charles, aged ten—and had a special message for fourteen-year-old Wally "to take good care of Mom."

Nowhere in the letter did he mention the coach's warning of possible trouble ahead. He certainly didn't want her worrying about it. Besides, it was trouble that might never come.

The next morning Spinks Pinley came to see him. The *Express* reporter was waiting outside the field-house when Scotty came out with the book of plays Coach Foster had given him.

"Won't take up much of your time, kid," Pinley said. "Just want to get acquainted." He was a large fleshy man, sloppily dressed with necktie askew. "So you're Clayburn, Mayville's Miracle Kid. Decided to move up to the Big Time, eh? Don't blame you. No percentage in wasting your talent in the sticks. No offense to the hometown, of course. Nice little town, Mayville. Guess they feel pretty sad about losing you. By the way, kid, how *did* they take it? No hard feelings—I hope?"

So that, Scotty thought, was the way Pinley operated. Assume things without even asking you. Leave you to deny them or agree by your silence. Either way he had you on the defensive.

And that first question—his only question so far—had probed about the sorest spot he could have picked.

Scotty didn't answer it. He said, "Mayville will get along all right. And I didn't leave because I thought I was 'wasting my talent.' I came to Westland High to get some vocational courses offered here."

Pinley laughed. "I can see you're a smart kid, Clayburn. But since you're here—to get all that education—you will play football, I take it." He chuckled as if he'd made a joke. "Yep, plenty of football, from what I hear. You're living up to your press notices already. Sort of gave the boys lessons yesterday, I understand, first time you laid a hand on the ball."

"I'm afraid you understand wrong, Mr. Pinley," Scotty said. "I'm the guy that'll be getting lessons around here. These boys play a fast brand of football."

Pinley grinned. "You're a sharp one, kid. Make it modest for the press. But you're not fooling me any. I know you're good—plenty good. Also know Westland needs a fancy ball toter like you. Haven't had a real breakaway runner in three years, and none in sight—until you showed up."

"Look, mister," Scotty broke in, "I'm in a sort of hurry. Have to make a class."

"Sure, kid. Wouldn't want to make a scholar late." He laughed again at his lame joke. Then his eyes narrowed. "Just one question, since you're in a hurry. To whom are we indebted for getting you interested in Westland High? I'd like to give our benefactor the proper credit for bringing us a star recruit."

Scotty fought to control a rising anger. "I've explained why I came to Westland. Maybe you didn't hear me."

"Okay, okay." Pinley shrugged. "Play it cagey. Didn't really expect you to answer that one. . . . Well, be seeing you around, kid." He waved airily and shuffled off.

Walking to the main building, Scotty thought it over. Pinley really hadn't interviewed him at all. The man's only questions had been more insinuations than questions. Pinley had done most of the talking, apparently figuring he already knew all the answers. Maybe he wasn't going to write a story. Maybe he really was just "getting acquainted," as he called it. It was something to hope for anyway.

Scotty had reached the second-floor hall when he heard someone call out his name. He turned. Over by some windows overlooking an inner court, Dave Franklin stood with a little knot of students. Dave motioned Scotty to join them.

"Want you to meet some folks," Dave said. He pointed them out. "Julie Fisher . . . Jim Harte . . . Eddie Skeen. Kids, this is Scotty Clayburn. He's from Mayville, and he's the kind of football player coaches dream about."

Scotty smiled, a little embarrassed. "Sure nice to meet all of you. And the build-up was slightly exaggerated."

"Modest as he is good," Dave said. Then, addressing Scotty, "Julie here is secretary of the Junior Class and a majorette. Jim is vice president of the Student Council. Eddie is sports editor of the *Zephyr,* school newspaper. Quite a collection of VIPs."

"From Mayville, are you?" Eddie Skeen was looking at Scotty with interest. The sports editor was a smallish boy with a keenly alert expression. "Say . . . you're the fellow that scored about three hundred points last year."

"What's that?" Dave's jaw dropped. "He didn't tell me—"

"Why don't you read the papers, Franklin?" Skeen said. "This guy broke so many records they threw the book away."

Julie Fisher spoke up. "Why, that's wonderful. Welcome to Westland, Scotty. We can always use a good football player."

Scotty liked the way she said it—not overdone, just friendly. She was a pretty girl too, he noticed. Blue-eyed, with smoothly tanned features and honey-colored hair. He said, "Don't take those records too seriously. That was Class A ball. Some of the competition wasn't so hot."

"Just the same," Julie replied, "I'm glad you'll be on our side Friday night."

"He can't play this season," Dave said.

"Why?" Julie asked innocently.

Jim Harte said, "Come now, Julie, don't tell me you never heard of the transfer rule. He has to attend school here a year before he's eligible for football."

"Lose a year?" Julie said. "That's a shame."

"It's a good rule," Eddie Skeen observed. "Stopped big towns from going out and stealing little towns' good ball players."

"Didn't stop all of it," Jim Harte said. "They tell me those oil men down at Concho have moved in about six families with a football star in each family. Watch out for that team next year!"

"Watch out for *that* team any year," Skeen said.

"Hey, you fellows," Julie broke in. "How about changing the subject? Jim, I was just thinking. You're on the program committee for the Welcome Assembly. Have you chosen your new-student speakers yet?"

"Nope." Jim grinned. "And I bet I know who you're going to suggest to represent the out-of-towners."

"Know anybody who'd be any better?" Julie challenged. "Scotty, it's like this. Friday we have our Welcome Assembly for new students. One feature of the program is speeches by three new students, one soph from each of the two junior highs and one new student who's moved in from out of town. You'll do it, won't you?"

"Well," Scotty demurred, "speaking is not exactly my long suit—"

"Good. I don't like orators anyway." Julie smiled. "You'll do fine, Scotty. Just make a three-minute talk— how it feels to be a newcomer at Westland, how you like the school and all that."

"Now just a minute, Julie," Jim Harte said. "Scotty suits me fine, but I'll have to check with the rest of the committee, just to make it official. Tell you what,

Scotty, the committee meets today or tomorrow, and I'll let you know."

"I still think you should get a better speaker"— Scotty saw the "please" in Julie's eyes—"but I'll give it a try."

"I'll let you know," Jim repeated. "I'm sure the others will okay it— Woop, there goes the old siren."

It was the warning bell, rung three minutes before the tardy signal. The group scattered to their various home rooms.

As Dave and Scotty walked together, Dave said with a grin, "You know, for a country-town boy, you're not doing so bad. You've been here one day and you already have a reputation as a ball player and an invite to make a speech at the first assembly. Boy, you're doing all right."

"Guess I got introduced to the right people." Scotty smiled. "No kidding, Dave, those folks were swell. I really didn't expect the kids in a big school to be so friendly."

"Why not? We're just like kids everywhere else. Just happen to be a lot of us."

As they went on down the long hall, thronged with students—hurrying, talking, laughing—Westland High somehow no longer seemed a strange place to Scotty Clayburn. Suddenly, he was beginning to feel he was a part of it.

It was a good feeling. He hoped nothing would happen to spoil it.

Chapter Six

The radio teacher's name was Ernest Bechtel. He was a tall, angular man with a calm, easy-going manner.

"In this course," he told the class, "lab activity will be the most vital phase of your work. I will assign lab partners, or you may choose your partner if you wish. I will give you a couple of days to decide."

They would spend most of the first six weeks studying basic electricity, he explained, then get into radio proper. They would build a one-tube receiver and, before the end of the term, a superheterodyne. They would also be going into television before the end of the year. He went on to give them a brief picture of the whole field of electronics.

Scotty could see already that this class would be all he'd hoped for. This teacher really knew his subject and had an enthusiasm that was stimulating.

When the time came for questions, Scotty asked, "Will we do any actual repair work on radio and TV sets?" The teacher replied that they would, later in the year. One of the class projects would be to bring in out-of-order sets and repair them in lab.

When the bell rang, the boy on Scotty's left turned with an impulsive gesture. "So you're in a hurry to start puttering with the family radio and TV, huh? Me, too. Have you ever done much of that?"

"I've tinkered a little," Scotty said, surprised at the sudden overture. "Just the simpler stuff, of course."

"I'm Bob Knowles," the boy said, holding out a hand. He was a short boy with a ready grin.

"Scotty Clayburn." Scotty took the hand. The warm grip fitted well with the boy's naturally open and friendly manner.

"I might be getting a little previous," Bob Knowles said, "but I've got a hunch you and I could work well as lab partners. Got anybody else in mind?"

"Not a soul. In fact, I don't even know anyone else in the class."

"Oh? New here?"

Scotty nodded. "Just moved to Westland."

"Well, if you want some time to think it over—"

"I've thought it over," Scotty replied. "If you want to take the risk, we'll call it a deal."

"It's a deal! Say, I'd like you to meet Phil Caudle."

A slender blond boy who'd been lingering beside

48

Bob Knowles stepped out and took Scotty's hand. "I'm giving you fair warning, Scotty, this Knowles is a radio nut. Stay away from him if you want to talk anything else."

"Look who's talking," Bob Knowles countered. "Phil and his partner, Esco Hammer, are ahead of us already. They built transistor sets this summer."

"Talking radio sure won't bother me any," Scotty said. "Wasn't it our old friend Emerson who said nothing was ever accomplished without enthusiasm—or something like that?"

"Could be, but don't ask me," Phil said. "That literature stuff bugs me."

"Which reminds me," Bob said. "I'm due at English in about two minutes."

"English this period?" said Scotty. "What teacher?"

"Stinson, in 205."

"Then we're in the same class."

"Swell!" Bob grinned. "Well, we better hit the road. Stinson takes a dim view of tardies."

He was an impulsive kid, Scotty thought, but he was okay. There was a lot of sincerity in that wide grin. It was a real stroke of luck getting a good partner like that in radio lab. In fact, Scotty reflected, finding new friends in this new school was turning out to be a lot easier than he'd ever expected.

In his study-hall period Scotty got out the book of plays Coach Foster had given him. Somebody had said the T formation was basically simple. That guy must have had a sense of humor, Scotty thought, as he waded through diagrams of handoffs, pitchouts, keepers, sneaks, crisscrosses, reverses, traps, counter plays—quarterback passes, running passes—then the flanker series, right and left.

But as he studied, basic patterns began to emerge. For example, stemming from the same design as the bread-and-butter handoff play came three other plays: the keeper, the running pitchout, and the running pass. All started the same way; only a simple variation in assignments was needed to change from one play to the other.

Coach Foster had told him: "For the present, consider yourself a left halfback. Learn your assignments on every play. Then start studying the other men's assignments. I like my backs to know what every man is doing on every play."

It was quite a task, but Scotty knew he could do it. Not so soon, though, would he learn how all that stuff looked and felt out there on the field—the actual execution, the mechanical detail. At Mayville he'd been pretty much of a one-man offense. Now he must learn to be a cog in a four-man offense. It would take time. He wouldn't master it in a week, or even two. But he was determined to master it before the season was over. He wanted to be in that first-string backfield next year.

He started work on it that afternoon. The basic play of the T was the handoff. He took advantage of handoff drill to work on every detail—proper stance, coming in "tall," inside leg on backward stride when he took the ball, "looking" the ball into his hands, speed on takeoff.

When it was over, he knew he'd made progress, but he was far from satisfied. He always liked to get everything perfect.

Group drills over, Jeffers called them together. Today the scrubs would test first-team defense by running the plays used by Fairdale, the Friday opponent.

Scotty watched. It was pretty one-sided. Fairdale's offense was similar to Westland's. The defense was familiar with the plays, and they were stopping them with a monotony that was disheartening to the outmanned scrubs.

After some twenty minutes, Jeffers called a pause and conferred with Foster. The backfield coach turned and called: "Clayburn—in here!" Scotty grabbed a red jersey.

Foster spoke to them in the huddle. "We're going to try those running passes again. Fairdale has a boy at left half who can throw well and can really scoot. I know you can throw, Clayburn. Do you know the play?"

"Yes, sir." Scotty was glad he'd studied those diagrams.

"Okay," Foster said. "Remember, the strength of the play lies in the fact that you can always turn it into a run. If the secondary pulls back too fast, take off. If they come in, pick your receiver and throw. I'll name the patterns. The deep pass this time."

Scotty knew it wasn't going to be easy. He knew the play on paper, yes. But running it would be something else. And he was facing that first string—smart, rugged boys who would be tough for the blockers to handle. Tough for *him,* too. Yesterday he'd had some advantage of surprise. Today it would be different.

The quarterback took the ball, and Scotty ran to the right. There was a fake to the right half, then the pitchout. The instant Scotty took the ball, he knew it wouldn't go. McGraw, playing left end on defense, was dumping the scrub fullback and looming right in Scotty's path. Keegan had broken through from tackle; Cowan was thundering in, and Gaddis, the middle backer, was right behind him. They converged on Scotty.

There was no receiver open. Scotty pulled in the ball and took his lumps. They ganged him. They hammered him to earth.

Cowan leered. "Looka who's here—little fancy Dan. Something tells me you're not going to be so fancy today."

In the huddle Foster said, "Pitiful blocking! Now let's try it again—and keep those guys out of there!"

The quarterback's pitchout went astray, and Scotty had to turn back for it. McGraw was blocking his path. Scotty tried to fade and look for a receiver. But too much time had been lost. Linemen were coming through. He danced away from two of them. And then Cowan rode him down.

The big boy jibed, "You're not doing so good, sonny. Maybe the game's getting a little rough, huh?"

Scotty ignored it. Cowan was very irritating, but he didn't want to disturb the workout with a squabble.

"Run a thirty-six," Foster sighed. "Give Clayburn a rest, then we'll try it once more."

The fullback hit off tackle for a yard, and they lined up for the running pass again. This time the pitchout was good; the blocks held fairly well. McGraw was still a menace, but Scotty managed to elude him and kept running wide. His eye photographed the action upfield: Cowan was playing for a run, closing in fast. Keegan and Gaddis were coming across. Leighton, at halfback, had come in momentarily but now had reversed to pick up the end. The end was open for a moment.

Scotty threw. In that same instant, Cowan leaped at him, elbows flailing. Scotty spun off his left foot, and Cowan grabbed empty air, stumbling to his knees. He got up, turning to Scotty with a crooked grin. "Kinda anxious to get rid of that thing, weren't you, Clayburn?"

"Sure," Scotty said. "Any time I can pick up thirty yards—" He stopped, staring in disappointment. The ball had fallen beyond the end's reach. He'd led him a fraction too much.

Jeffers, apparently, thought differently. He was lecturing the defense. "There it is. Let 'em do that Friday and it's a touchdown. A fast end would have had that and been gone."

The scrubs ran it again. This time Keegan burst through. McGraw manhandled the fullback. The two of them bruised in on Scotty. Cowan was holding back, however, immobilized for the moment by the right half, a potential receiver. Leighton was sticking with the end downfield.

Scotty moved with the speed of a darting shadow. He

53

hit the crack of daylight between Keegan and Mc-Graw, and neither man touched him. He dug two more strides, then cut to his right. Cowan, recovering quickly, made his bid. Scotty feinted as if to cut back, then pulled wider with a new flash of speed. He left Cowan clawing the turf.

Leighton maneuvered warily, guarding the sideline. Hodges moved over, closing the opening. Allred, led far astray by the decoy left end, was coming back fast. The scrub right end tried to become a blocker, but Leighton fended him off, dumped him. Scotty cut back sharply, running straight at Hodges, freezing him. A pace away from the tackler, he sidestepped, straight-arm extended. Hodges came in low, under the straight-arm, his shoulder splatting into Scotty's right leg.

Scotty let the leg go limp. Hodges went down, his grasp weakening, but still holding the ankle. Scotty did a hitch-kick, and the leg came free. He stumbled, regained stride, and was gone, with Allred in hot pursuit. Jeffers' whistle screeched.

"Six more points for Fairdale," the coach sang out.

He called his team together. "That 5–3–2–1 will stop that running pass option if you play it smart. You did everything right that time—except the tackling. I know, that boy is pretty elusive. You had to get under the straight-arm, Hodges, but not that low. These tricky runners have a way of getting away from those low tackles. And, Cowan, remember. You don't watch a shifty man's shoulders or eyes; you watch his legs."

"I had to cover the receiver," Cowan sulked. "What

54

about McGraw and Keegan? They could have had him for a loss."

"*You* should have had him," Jeffers said, with just a trace of sharpness. "He foxed you with one of the oldest tricks in the book. We all make mistakes, Cowan. But we learn by admitting them and correcting them. . . . Okay, men, let's get in there and stop that stuff."

"The X-pass this time," Foster told the scrubs.

They were fired up, inspired by their sudden success against the regulars. The fullback put a solid shoulder block on McGraw, tying him up momentarily. Scotty ran wide, studying the pattern ahead. Cowan was coming up fast. The decoys were doing a nice job—right half flaring into the flat, right end slanting deep to the left. The left end made his turn, sharp to the right, and he was free in the zone vacated by Cowan. Scotty feathered the ball into the end's hands.

And then Cowan hit him.

Scotty was not expecting it. He'd already thrown, and instinctively he figured Cowan would check his charge. But Cowan came on, and Scotty was off guard. He had a sensation of bone-jarring impact, then something exploded against his jaw, and all sensation dissolved into black nothingness.

When he woke up, he was still on the ground. Foster was bent over him. "Try moving your jaw—easy, kid!"

Scotty smiled rather feebly. "I'm okay. Just knocked out for a minute, I guess."

Foster sighed relief. "You must have an iron jaw, son. Seems to be in one piece all right." He motioned two boys to help Scotty up.

55

"I'm okay, Coach," Scotty insisted. "Let's get on with the scrimmage."

"Not you," Jeffers said. "Sit down over there and take a rest." There was something in the head coach's eyes Scotty had not seen there before—cold, outright anger.

Jeffers turned to Cowan, his voice barely audible. "Cowan, have I ever coached you to slam an elbow into the passer's face?"

"It was accidental," Cowan said, sullenly. "I was just trying to break up the throw."

"He'd already thrown the ball. He was out of the play. We're practicing football—not deliberate roughing."

Cowan's temper flamed. *"He* can play football, but I've got to play tag. How'd he get to be a privileged character so quick!"

Jeffers said softly, "Nobody is a privileged character around here, Cowan—and that includes you." He paused, his eyes hard on the fullback. "Is that clear?"

Cowan's eyes dropped. "Yes, sir. I understand."

They resumed scrimmage, but plainly the incident had upset their concentration. A few minutes later, Jeffers sent them in.

It seemed to be a day for "incidents." Another happened in the dressing room. Chigger Rambo was going down the aisle picking up used towels. The little fellow was darting here and there, working hurriedly as usual.

And then it happened. It was a small thing, almost nothing. But Cowan was still in a nasty mood, and that made the difference. Cowan, coming from the shower, was striding behind Rambo. And suddenly Rambo, seeing a towel lying under a bench, backed up with a quick movement and stooped to pick it up. Cowan stumbled over him and sprawled to the floor.

It was not a bad fall. Cowan had thrown out his hands, cushioning the shock. But he came up glowering at Rambo. "You stupid little ape! What're you trying to do—cripple me!"

Rambo's face flamed darkly, but he answered calmly. "Sorry. I didn't see you. It was an accident."

"Yeh? I bet you did it on purpose." Cowan advanced on Rambo, raising an open hand in a menacing gesture.

Scotty was suddenly between them, pushing Rambo gently aside, putting himself in front of Cowan. "Take it easy, Cowan. You're all excited over nothing. He told you it was an accident."

"What's it to *you!*" Cowan raged. "This is none of your business. And get out of my way before I clout you!"

At that instant several others arrived. Somebody grabbed Cowan. Dave Franklin said, "Don't be a dunce, Cowan. You want Coach to suspend you from the squad?"

Cowan's rage-filled eyes sobered a little. Jeffers would not tolerate any brawling in the dressing room.

Somebody said, "What started all this anyway?"

Chigger spoke up. "It's my fault. I accidentally tripped Cowan and he got mad, and Scotty—"

Cowan broke in. "Aw, I was just kidding Rambo, and Clayburn had to horn in and make something serious out of it. Guess I kind of blew my stack at Clayburn for getting me all wrong. I'm sorry." The big boy's expression had changed suddenly. He was wearing a forced grin. "I'm willing to forget the whole thing if he is."

The others looked at Scotty. Scotty looked at Cowan, puzzled by his sudden change of front. Then he got it. Plainly, Cowan had realized that this business was about to put him in a bad light. Now he was trying to cast doubt in the minds of the others, make them wonder if maybe Scotty had been a little hasty.

Scotty said, "That's okay with me."

Dave spoke up then. "Why don't we all get some clothes on and get out of here?" He laughed, trying to ease the tension.

They broke up, and to all outward appearances the incident was closed.

But Scotty knew it wasn't. Cowan wasn't going to forget. From now on, he feared, the big fullback was his enemy for sure.

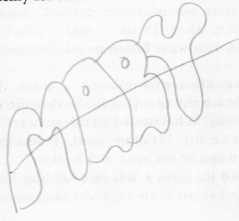

Chapter
Seven

Scotty worked on his speech that night. They hadn't notified him "officially" yet, but he wanted to be prepared anyway. He would write it that night; the next two nights he could practice speaking it.

The big house was very quiet. His uncle had left town on a business trip, and his aunt had gone out for the evening with some friends.

He started scribbling. "Fellow students of Westland High, I feel highly honored to represent all those who have moved here from out of town to make this their new school home—"

He stopped a moment, looked at it, then crumpled the paper and threw it into the wastebasket. Too stiff and formal. He wanted to say something simple and sincere. Because, already, he had a sincere feeling about this school. If he could just put it into words. . . .

For an hour he wrote and revised and threw away and rewrote. Finally, he made a fresh copy and read it over. Not so bad. Maybe not so much of a speech, but it honestly expressed his real pride in becoming a part of a great school. He read it aloud slowly, timing himself. Three minutes, almost exactly.

He was still scared at the idea of walking up to the mike, facing a vast auditorium full of students. But he'd been asked to do it, and he wanted to do his best. He'd hate Julie Fisher to regret she'd suggested him.

Next morning on his way to first-period class, he took a short cut through the court. The ground-level court was styled as a patio, with cactus and Spanish dagger and other such planting. It was open on the south and could be entered by big doors on the other three sides of the U-shaped building. Students were scattered about the court, grabbing a chance for some conversation before classes.

Scotty noticed a group in one corner, among them Dave and Eddie Skeen and Jim Harte. Also Fred Gaddis, first-string center on the team. He drifted over to join them. Jim might have some word for him from the assembly program committee.

Dave said, "Hi, Scotty." He introduced three boys. "You know the others of course."

"Sure do," Scotty said affably. He cast an inquiring glance at Jim Harte, but Jim said nothing.

60

In fact, nobody was saying anything. And all at once Scotty sensed something strange here. They'd been talking at a fast clip when he came up. Now an odd silence had settled over them.

Dave spoke then. "No home room today, Scotty. Guess you know."

"Yeh," Scotty said. "Well, I better move along."

He walked away, vaguely disturbed. Maybe he was just being oversensitive. But he couldn't rid himself of the feeling that he'd interrupted something back there; and whatever it was, they definitely didn't want him to hear it.

He ran into Bob Knowles outside the radio classroom. With Bob was a small youth with keen dark eyes.

"Hey, Scotty," Bob greeted him. "If you ever want to buy a transistor kit, let me know. I found a place where we can get a discount." Then, without pausing, "This runt is Esco Hammer, the scientific brain of the school. Esco, this is Scotty Clayburn, the guy I told you about."

"Huh?" Esco said absently.

"My new lab partner, you dope."

"Oh, yeh. Hiya, Clayburn," Esco said.

"Glad to meet you, Esco," Scotty replied.

"Speaking of dopes," Esco said to Scotty, "you've got one for a lab partner. He talks a great experiment, but you'll have to do all the work."

"Down, boy," Bob growled with mock severity. "Say, Scotty, you held out on us yesterday. Didn't tell us you were a football star."

"Let's say I'm working out with the squad," Scotty said. Funny, he thought, how quickly things got around.

"The way I heard it," Bob said, "you're a lot more than just another man on the squad. Too bad you can't play this year." He explained to Esco, "Scotty being a transfer, he'll have to attend here a year before he's eligible."

"I know the rule," Esco said without enthusiasm.

Bob grinned. "Esco's not much of a football fan."

"Football," Esco said matter-of-factly, "is greatly overemphasized. Especially in this school."

"Don't mind him, Scotty," Bob said. "He makes weird statements now and then, but he's basically harmless."

"No personal offense intended, Clayburn," Esco said, with the same deadpan expression. "Some rather intelligent fellows play football, though sometimes I wonder for what reason."

"I'll give you some reasons sometime, Esco," Scotty said good-naturedly. "Right now we better get into that class—before that bell stops ringing."

It was the second period. Miss Stinson had just finished checking the roll when Julie Fisher came into the room and handed the English teacher a slip of paper. Scotty tried to catch Julie's eye and felt somehow disappointed when she didn't look in his direction.

"Scotty Clayburn."

62

The teacher's voice startled him. He walked to the front. Miss Stinson held out the slip and said, "Call slip. It will explain itself."

Scotty read it and got another minor shock. It read: "Please send Scotty Clayburn to the Principal's Office at once."

Julie was waiting in the hall. She said, "The only slip I had to deliver this trip. Thought I might as well wait and see you didn't get lost on the way to the office."

"Nice to have an official escort." Scotty smiled. "So you work in the office this period."

She nodded. "Sort of errand girl. Have you got that speech ready yet?"

"I've given it some thought. Of course, I haven't heard from the committee yet."

"Oh, you can count on it." Julie smiled with a confidential air. "It's unofficial, but I happen to know they met and okayed you unanimously."

"Just hope my mind doesn't go blank when I face that audience."

"I'm not worrying," Julie said. "Oh, wanted to tell you. Joan Cantrell, one of our seniors, is planning a party soon. Her folks own a ranch about twenty miles out. Fabulous place. She invites lots of kids out every fall. There's dancing, horseback riding, games, whatever you like. And tons of old-fashioned pit barbecue. Be sure and go. You'll meet a lot of kids."

"That'd be swell—if I get invited, of course."

"You'll be invited," Julie said. "She always has the

football players out. She picks some Saturday when there's a day off from practice."

Scotty felt much better now. Perhaps the call to the office was about some routine detail, maybe his transcript of grades.

Julie seemed to have read his thoughts. "Don't let that slip worry you. Discipline cases go to the assistant principal. You'll probably never get acquainted with him."

"Thanks for your confidence," Scotty said, laughing.

They entered the outer office. Julie said, "Give me the slip and I'll hand it to the secretary."

The secretary, at a desk inside an enclosure, looked at the slip and lifted an interoffice phone. "Scotty Clayburn, Mr. Kenwood." She racked the phone. "Mr. Kenwood will see you at once. Just open the door and go in."

The moment Scotty walked into the private office, he knew it wasn't just some routine detail.

Charles Kenwood, a tall, spare man, was seated behind a broad desk, a grave expression on his lean face. But it wasn't the principal who gave Scotty a sudden feeling of alarm. It was the fact that another man was seated in the room—Coach Jeffers. And though the coach shot Scotty a brief smile of greeting, he too wore a sober look.

"Have a seat, Scotty." The principal's tone was kindly.

"As you may have guessed—since Mr. Jeffers is here with us—I have called you in on a matter relating to your participation in football." Mr. Kenwood picked up a newspaper from his desk. "But before we go into any discussion, have you read yesterday's *Express?*"

"No, sir," Scotty said, his heart thumping with an unwelcome premonition.

"Hmm. Perhaps it would be a good idea for you to read the article I have marked there." He handed the paper over the desk.

"You mean—now, sir?"

"Now," the principal said. "Don't feel hurried. Take time to read it all."

It was the sports page of *The Evening Express.* A red-penciled line marked the title of Spinks Pinley's column, "Spinks' Sports Sparks."

Scotty read:

Well, folks, it looks as if the old Touchdown Club, driven underground some years ago, may be coming to life again. The Touchdown Club, remember, was a group of downtown tycoons who made it their business to insure Westland a winning football team each year. Their method was quite simple—any time the crop of home-grown hopefuls looked a little thin, they'd scout around and bring in some imported talent. The system worked right well—or have you forgotten those golden years of undefeated teams?

The state committee sort of stifled the T.D. boys with the transfer rule. But they still brought in a lad now and then and kept him on ice a year till he was eligible. Then, six years ago, a new regime came in—and the T.D. Club went out. Wouldn't tolerate no such shenanigans, the new coach and administration said.

Now comes a new development. Could be the long

arm of coincidence, but we'll give you some facts. Every football filbert knows the crying need of the Tigers is a climax runner, a real breakaway boy who's liable to go all the way any time. We haven't had one lately, and from the looks of the material coming up, we weren't going to have one any time soon.

Well, folks, we've got one now. A neat little package of football goods named Scotty Clayburn, and he's a climax runner from way back. Played last year for Mayville, a little hamlet about 120 miles northwest, and he did everything up there but take up tickets. Broke loose 23 times for T.D. jaunts of 50 to 96 yards. He had two more years to go up there, and you can bet your Sunday shirt the fans at Mayville were mighty glad of it. But he's not at Mayville any more, dear readers; he's right here in old Westland High, where he enrolled Monday and worked out with the ball club.

One angle is a little strange, though. His family didn't move to Westland with him.

Of course the big question is, How come this boy suddenly gets interested in Westland High? Could be the kid decided educational advantages were better than Mayville's. That's what the lad himself says. But on some other points he's not so definite. Asked if anybody helped sell him on the virtues of Westland, he just plain dodged the question. On the topic of what the hometown folks thought about his departure, he refused to comment. We were hoping he could truthfully deny some reports we've been getting, because these reports are sort of distressing, namely, that the folks at Mayville are hopping mad and are saying somebody came along and waved some

66

"inducements" around and lured their boy to the big town.

Now, we're not trying to persecute the boy. He seems like a smart, clean-cut kid, and if there's any hanky-panky going on, he probably doesn't actually realize it. But the way he parried our questions sure looks like he'd been well briefed.

So, like we said, maybe the old Touchdown Club is coming to life again—or maybe some old members are on the job individually. If that's the case, we'll say one thing: they've got a foolproof setup this time. This boy is living with John Durham, and John Durham is his uncle—and how can anybody make it their business if an uncle wants to help his nephew?

Still, it looks like somebody has decided to help Westland have another state champion next year. We're not saying it's such a bad idea. Personally, we're looking forward to watching this kid do his stuff in the Westland backfield next fall.

But you have to admit it's a little tough on Mayville.

Scotty laid the newspaper on the desk and said nothing. There was a lot he'd like to say, but he figured he'd better save it till he was called on.

Jeffers said, "We know, Scotty, that no matter what you said in the interview, Pinley twisted it around."

"Yes," the principal agreed. "The man is very skillful at distorting facts. Unfortunately, though, many people like his column and believe what he writes, or insinuates. You can see that this sort of publicity is not good for our athletic situation. I believe Coach Jeffers

67

has explained to you our policy on so-called recruiting."

Scotty nodded. "Yes, sir."

"The coach tells me you came here for some vocational work not offered at Mayville." Mr. Kenwood's eyes narrowed. "Was that your only reason for changing schools?"

"Yes, sir, it was."

"Were you not also attracted to Westland by the prospect of playing football here?"

Scotty hesitated a moment. "If I understand the question—no, sir."

Mr. Kenwood polished his glasses. "Let's go at it another way. Mr. Jeffers has told me something you probably don't know. For more than a year your uncle tried to get Mr. Jeffers to extend you—we'll say an 'unofficial invitation' to move here and play football. Naturally, Mr. Jeffers refused."

Scotty stiffened. This *was* something he hadn't known.

"And now," Mr. Kenwood said, "it appears that Mr. Durham went ahead on his own and induced you to come."

"No, sir," Scotty said. "It was my own idea."

The principal's piercing eyes were fixed on Scotty. "Think carefully. Isn't it just possible that your idea grew from some subtle suggestions made by your uncle?"

Scotty smiled for the first time. "There wasn't anything subtle about his suggestions, sir. He'd just come

68

out and say, 'Why don't you move down and live with us and play football on a big-time team.' "

Mr. Kenwood blinked. "And that didn't influence you?"

"Not a bit. But when he happened to mention the courses, I did get interested. You can ask Uncle John about all this. He'd tell you."

Jeffers spoke up. "We tried to get hold of your uncle and have him meet with us, but he's out of town." Then he added, "We're not trying to question your honesty, Scotty. Mr. Kenwood just wants to be sure of the facts. Pinley's article has put us in a vulnerable spot."

Mr. Kenwood cleared his throat. "It's a bit hard to explain, Scotty. Legally, we're in the clear. But we want to follow the spirit of the rules, not merely the letter. So it all comes down to motive—*what* induced you to transfer. You may feel that this is your own business, that we are meddling in a private matter between you and your uncle. The trouble is, Scotty, you are a public figure, and your private business becomes public business. It shouldn't be that way, but it is. What you do not only involves you; it involves the school, the whole town. I repeat, it's not fair to you boys to be put under this pressure by overzealous football fans, but that's how it is. Too many people look upon you as public property."

The man was leading up to something, Scotty sensed. And he had a feeling it wouldn't be good.

"We're glad to have you here as a student," the principal resumed. "I see by your transcript that you have a B-plus average, with A's in math and science. Mr. Jeffers has been impressed with your personal qualities. But your playing football poses a problem." He paused for a deep breath. "The simplest solution, as I see it, would be for you to voluntarily drop out of football."

Scotty paled. So that was it—the blow he'd been dreading.

The principal was talking again. "Perhaps you feel this is more than we should ask you to sacrifice. On the other hand, you must realize that if you do play, you will face some personal difficulties. You will be subject to criticism and suspicion. This fellow Pinley has sown the seed, and he'll write other things to keep it alive. That is his way of getting readers. . . . So, what is your choice? Or do you want to think it over awhile?"

Scotty looked at Jeffers. Something in the coach's expression said: *Stick it out. I'll stand by you.*

Scotty said, "I don't want to cause any trouble, sir. But if the choice is left to me—I'll play football."

Kenwood regarded him gravely. "All right, son. But you must remember one thing. Everything you do will be spotlighted in the pitiless glare of publicity. Your conduct in every way must always be above reproach." The principal stood and held out a hand. "Good luck. I hope you have a good year in school."

Scotty stood and shook the proffered hand. "Thank you, sir."

Outside the office, Jeffers said, "Don't hold it against him for giving you the third degree. He gets put on the spot same as other folks. He had a call from a board member this morning, and he had to be sure where he stood."

"I understand," Scotty said. "I guess, at that, it was pretty nice of him to give me a choice."

Jeffers smiled a little grimly. "If he hadn't been convinced you were telling the truth, Scotty, you wouldn't have had any choice."

Scotty was thoughtful. "There was one thing about that column I couldn't figure. He kept harping on the Touchdown Club—those men who brought in players. That was years ago. What's that got to do with me now?"

Jeffers was silent a long moment. "Scotty, you're going to find out something, and I'd rather you learned it from me. There's probably no more than a handful of people who would have remembered it, but now Pinley's column will start talk—and it will be all over town. That stuff was Pinley's way of getting in an underhand dig at your uncle. . . . You see, John Durham was a very active member of the old Touchdown Club."

Chapter
Eight

Scotty stood stunned for a moment before his mind could accept what Jeffers had just told him.

Then he saw the full import of it. The insinuations Pinley had written might be discounted by some people. But this was different. Here was a fact no one could deny. John Durham, in the past, had had a part in "buying" players from little towns. Now John Durham's nephew had left a little town to play for Westland. It wasn't hard to see the conclusion a lot of people would draw from that.

He remembered what the boys had said back in Mayville: "Can't blame a guy for taking a better thing." . . . "Wonder how much he's getting to play for them."

Would they be saying the same things now in Westland?

Another depressing thought struck him. He wondered—would his uncle have offered him a home and a chance to attend Westland High if he had not been a football player? In the next instant he felt guilty at the thought. Sure, Uncle John had a big interest in football. But Uncle John was also interested in helping him get the training he wanted for his future. He was sure of it.

He turned to the coach. "I can see now the spot you're in. Maybe, after all—" He broke off, seeing the look in Jeffers' eyes. "Sorry. Like you said, running away from it isn't the right answer."

"Good boy!" Jeffers gripped Scotty's arm. "Go on back to your class now and try to forget this business. Promise?"

Scotty smiled soberly. "Thanks. I'll try."

Forgetting, he found, wasn't easy. He remembered the incident in the patio that morning. Eddie Skeen, the sportswriter, was sure to have read Pinley's column. Perhaps some of the others had too. Maybe they'd been discussing it, then clammed up when they saw Scotty approaching. It would figure.

On the way to lunch he passed Jim Harte. He was almost sure Jim saw him. Yet, when he spoke, Jim was suddenly looking the other way. It was a small thing he would have passed off the day before without a thought. Today, though, he wondered.

That afternoon he hurried to the locker room and

was putting on his pads when Dave and Rex Cowan arrived.

"Boy, are you the eager one!" Dave said.

Cowan said, "He can't wait to get out there and show us how. Pinley says he's the world's greatest ball player, and he probably believes it."

Nobody else made any cracks. But on the field Scotty sensed a subtle change in the atmosphere—a sort of aloofness. Yesterday they'd been friendly in a casual, easy manner. Today they just didn't seem to notice he was around. One thing sure, they'd read the column or had heard about it—and it had certainly done nothing to raise his rating with them.

The workout, for him, was a light one. They finished with a long dummy scrimmage in which he had no part. Later, when he'd showered and dressed, he walked to the bus stop in front of the main building. The setting sun was splashing vivid hues on the low-hanging clouds in the western sky. The merest hint of coming autumn touched the evening air. For a moment the unhappy events of the day receded. Scotty felt an exhilaration at the thought of the approaching autumn—the clear, cool, almost windless days of West Texas' best season.

His thoughts broke off. The long black Cadillac was pulling in at the curb. He hadn't expected Uncle John back until tomorrow.

As he stepped toward the car he had a glimpse of some of the players following on the walk behind him. Then voices:

74

"Look at that, you clods. Limousine service he gets —in a Caddy, no less."

"I've got a rich uncle in San Antonio. Wonder if I could get a deal like that."

"Sure. Just score forty touchdowns this year, and you'll have it made."

Scotty didn't look back. Just joking? Maybe. But their laughter left an unpleasant ring in his ears as he shut the car door.

"Glad I caught you before the bus came," his uncle said. "I finished my business in Dallas sooner than I expected and drove back this afternoon. Well, how's everything?"

"Oh"—Scotty hesitated—"pretty good." He should tell his uncle, of course, about the call to the principal's office. But somehow the words wouldn't come.

"Kid, something's bothering you and I think I know what. I stopped in town just now and saw a copy of the *Express*." John Durham chuckled. "Meant to warn you. Have to be careful what you say to that guy."

"I was careful. He got most of his stuff from somewhere else."

"Mostly out of his imagination, the louse. Don't let it upset you, Scotty. I was hoping Pinley would play it decent for once and give you some nice publicity. But he just can't resist the habit of trying to smear somebody. Anyway, forget it. Folks know he's always faking some hot inside dope. They read his stuff for kicks, but they don't take it seriously."

Not take it seriously? What about the school princi-

pal? The fellows on the squad? A lot of people, Scotty feared, were going to take it very seriously.

"The *Express* is a rag anyhow," his uncle was saying. "The *Times* is the real paper here. I talked to Clint Carlton, the sports editor. He'll probably give you a nice story before long."

Scotty said nothing. He doubted if anything he said could convince his uncle that the less publicity he got, the better. In fact, he was feeling a strange reluctance to confide in Uncle John at all. He'd postpone any mention of the call to the office, he decided. Somehow the whole business had become a touchy subject to discuss with his uncle.

One thing he couldn't help noticing. In all the conversation Uncle John had made no comment on Pinley's reference to the old Touchdown Club. . . .

Scotty was on his way to the lunchroom the next day when Jim Harte hailed him in the hall. "I've been trying to see you for a couple of days," Jim said. "About that speech—" He stopped a moment, as if he'd forgotten what he was going to say. He started again. "You remember, the one we were talking about for tomorrow's assembly?"

"Yeh, sure," Scotty said. Did he remember! He'd spent an hour last night practicing on it.

"Well," Jim blurted, "I was a little late with my suggestion. Other members of the committee had already contacted a boy, and he'd agreed to make the speech."

Scotty felt suddenly cold inside. He remembered

what Julie had said: ". . . unofficial, of course, but I happen to know the committee met and okayed you unanimously."

"Seems this other guy has quite a rep as a speaker," Jim was saying. "Big debater at his old school. Anyway, they'd heard about him and already latched on to him for the job."

"I see," Scotty said dully. "Thanks for letting me know."

He walked away, feeling a sort of numbness. Jim had been lying, of course. Oh, Julie could have been mistaken; only Scotty knew, deep down, that she wasn't. They had picked him to be on the program all right—then had changed their minds and marked him off. Somebody had read Pinley's article. And they'd decided that maybe this Clayburn wasn't the kind of fellow who should represent the new transfers to Westland High.

He should have suspected this would happen. Maybe, far back in his mind, he'd been expecting it. But somehow he hadn't been ready for it—and it hurt.

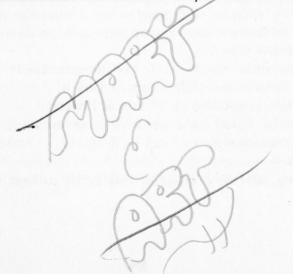

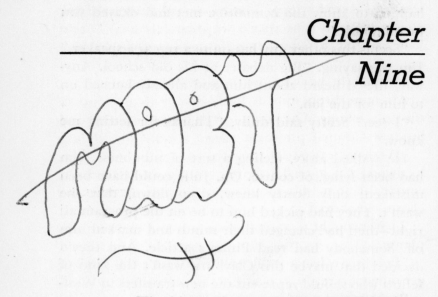

Chapter
Nine

The big auditorium echoed with the shuffle of feet and the hum of voices as three thousand students filed in and took their seats. The crimson curtains swept back, revealing a mammoth stage. Seated behind the footlights were some fifteen students. In the background was a giant banner, a crimson tiger on a field of white.

It was quite a picture, Scotty thought. He felt lost in the sea of unfamiliar faces, a little dazzled by all this, his first assembly at Westland High.

He'd be dazed for sure if he were up there now sitting on that stage!

He was no longer bitter about it. He'd done a lot of thinking, and he'd made up his mind to that. The suspicions stirred by Pinley were too absurdly groundless to hold up for long. These kids had a normal sense of fair play. In time they'd see their mistake. They'd look back on the whole thing as a silly misunderstanding.

Meanwhile, he was here to enjoy this assembly.

Applause broke out as Fred Gaddis stepped up to the microphone. The sandy-haired football captain and Student Council president raised a hand for silence.

"We have a two-part program today," he said. "Mr. Kenwood has agreed to give us some extra time. Of course, it may disappoint you to have first-period classes cut short."

That brought a round of laughter and more applause.

"Before we leave we'll hold our first pep rally—to get our team ready to beat Fairdale tonight."

Prolonged cheers interrupted him again.

Gaddis finally quieted them. "But before that, we are here to welcome the new students to our school. . . ."

There were speakers and more speakers. They explained the clubs, honorary societies, scholastic awards, publications, music activities, athletics, traditions. They gave a welcome to those from each of the junior highs, and each time a response was given by a sophomore. Then came a welcome to those who had moved in from out of town.

"And now, from Bardston, representing our out-of-town newcomers—Sumpter Bradley."

Scotty straightened in his seat.

The guy was probably a debater all right, he decided as he listened. It was a nice speech. Well worded and well delivered. *Better than I could have done,* Scotty told himself. He joined in the storm of applause as the speaker finished.

The speakers filed off the stage, and cheerleaders came bounding out amid an explosion of cheers. The head leader announced a yell, and the squad—four boys and four girls—went into action.

Crimson and white!
Crimson and white!
Yeaaaa, Tigers—
Fight! Fight! Fight!

Scotty had never heard anything like the noise. It was deafening.

The rally was short. Just a warm-up rally for a warm-up game, Scotty guessed. But it was loud while it lasted. No wonder the Tigers were famed for their will-to-win spirit!

He left the auditorium with a good warm feeling. Someday he'd really be a part of all this.

He felt a little tug at his arm. It was Julie Fisher. "Sorry I gave you the wrong dope, Scotty." She smiled ruefully. "I'm afraid my inside sources of information on committee meetings aren't so reliable."

Scotty caught it at once. Julie was trying to cover up, simply because she was the kind who hated to see anyone hurt or embarrassed. "Oh, that's okay." He smiled. "Say, I'm looking forward to seeing you perform tonight. You majorettes ready to give us a good show?"

"We'd better be—after practicing baton routines all summer." She waved a hand. "Got to hurry. Be seeing you."

There was a fresh spring in Scotty's step as he continued down the hall.

In the radio classroom Bob Knowles said, "How'd you like the pep rally, Scotty?" With Bob were the other two boys Scotty had met, Phil Caudle and Esco Hammer.

"Great!" Scotty said. "These kids really bring down the roof. Best organized cheering I ever heard."

"If you ask me," Esco said, "it's an awful lot of fuss over a ball game."

"Nobody asked you," said Bob.

"Okay, so nobody asked me," Esco countered. "I say we overdo it, that's all. We don't get all hopped up over other things kids do to represent the school. You ever hear of holding a pep rally for a debate team?"

Phil chuckled. "Esco probably wants a pep rally for him when he goes to district meet in slide rule."

Esco scowled. "Don't be an idiot. I'm just saying—"

"Knock it off, Esco," Bob interrupted. "I want to ask Scotty about those drawings on the voltmeter—"

But the teacher's voice, requesting their attention, cut off further conversation.

Scotty was thinking: Funny guy, Esco Hammer. Was he just the kind of kid who liked to start arguments by being "different"? Or did Esco really have what he considered an honest grudge against football? If so, what was behind it?

Moments later he'd dismissed the matter from his

mind. He was listening closely as Mr. Bechtel launched into an explanation of electrical resistance.

Scotty went out to the game that night. It was a non-league game against a mediocre ball club. Yet the concrete stands, which would hold more than twenty thousand, were half filled. Westland fans liked to see their boys play ball.

Uncle John took him to the box seats. He'd rather have sat in the student section, but he'd deferred to his uncle's wishes. "Want you to see this first one from the best seats, kid," Uncle John had said.

But another motive was soon apparent. Before the game began, he led Scotty around, introducing him to a dozen or so men. Hearty, bluff-voiced men. Mostly oil operators, Scotty figured, with a sprinkling of ranchmen. To each of them his uncle made a remark something like, "Yep, this is the boy. Wait'll he gets out there. You'll see some fancy ball totin'."

So that was it. Uncle John wanted to show him off and brag. It was embarrassing.

Scotty paid little notice to what the men said. Except one—a big man with beetle brows and a gravelly voice. "Star ball toter, eh?" he croaked. "Reminds me of the old days, John."

A little sharply, John Durham said, "None of that, King. This kid is my nephew."

The big man laughed. "Anyway, we got 'em some ball players, didn't we?"

John Durham quickly pushed Scotty on up the aisle. But Scotty kept thinking about the man with the gravelly voice. What was his name? . . . Carruth. King Carruth.

It was a name he would later have cause to remember.

The game began. Westland took the kickoff and started marching. Allred wide for eight. Cowan through the middle for five. Hodges off tackle for six.

It was pretty to watch, even though it was apparent the opposition wasn't too tough. Behind crisp blocking that ripped great holes in the Fairdale line, Westland backs tore off great chunks of yardage. They scored in nine plays.

Two minutes later Allred circled end and breezed 57 yards to another touchdown. It became a rout. At the end of the quarter it was 28–0, and Jeffers sent in the second string. It was 41–0 at the half.

As the teams left the field, John Durham said, "Scotty, you can move faster in this crowd than I can." He handed over a dollar bill. "How about running down to the concession stand and getting me a hot dog and black coffee? Get whatever you like for yourself."

Again Scotty was disappointed. He wanted to see the halftime show. Especially Julie Fisher with the majorettes. He'd hurry. Maybe he could get back in time to see most of it.

But a long line had already formed when he reached the concession booths beneath the stands. Scotty fell in at the end, wishing the line would move faster.

Suddenly, he was aware of the conversation of some men just behind him.

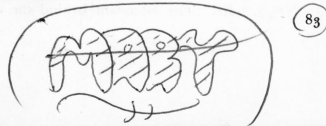

"Looking good for a season opener, aren't they?"

"Ought to take district in a breeze. Half of 'em will be back next year too. With that kid from Mayville in there, they should be a cinch for state. They say that kid is a whizzer."

"They look good to me just as they are. I don't see why we need to go out of town for football players."

"You and me," a third voice joined in. "We've been doing all right with Westland boys. We don't need to start shopping around for football tramps."

There was a laugh from the second voice. "Still, why waste that kind of talent on a tank-town ball club? If we can get a kid like that to move in here and play—why not?"

"Yeh? Remember what happened the last time we imported a bunch of goons? That Butch Bailey that played tackle—he got into a knifing scrape out at some honky-tonk. I say keep the team clean of that sort of riffraff."

"That Bailey could play ball though. How that guy could block! I'll never forget that state championship game at Bayport. He manhandled a whole side of Bayport's line."

"Yeh, I remember that game. They said the Touchdown Club boys carried a hundred grand out of Bayport after that one."

"Probably exaggerated, but they brought back plenty. I remember King Carruth drove down there in a brand-new Lincoln. Put the Lincoln up against five thousand—"

"Okay, fella!" The attendant behind the counter

84

was barking at Scotty. "Let's snap it up. What'll it be?"

Jeffers emptied the bench in the second half. The regulars stayed only long enough to score one quick touchdown and they were through for the night. The seconds took over and drove for another one. Jeffers promptly put in the third string.

Fairdale scored once, on a running pass against the fourth string late in the game. The final score was 54–6.

But Scotty saw little of what was going on in that second half. His mind was too full of troubled thoughts, of questions he couldn't answer.

Why was it that some people couldn't enjoy this wonderful game of football for what it was—a clean, hard battle of brawn and heart and skill? Why must they tarnish the bright thrill of it with something that was not quite clean?

His mind kept echoing the things he'd overheard: "Goons . . . riffraff . . . carried a hundred grand out of Bayport" . . .

And he kept wondering how many times that same talk—always including a reference to the new kid from Mayville—was being repeated all over town.

He knew the answer to that one, he feared.

Chapter Ten

On Monday Coach Foster said to Scotty, "I want you to practice running T quarterback. Montclair, our next opponent, has a boy who's good on the keeper play. You'll impersonate him against the first string."

Scotty practiced it. For fifteen minutes he drilled on taking the snapback, concentrating on the points Foster had given him: "Stand tall . . . hands close . . . throw that shoulder . . ."

"Still a little rough, but you'll improve," Foster said. "Now we'll drill on the handoff and pitchout." He enlisted other backs from the scrubs, and they went through the plays.

The next day he gave them a line and they worked

again, adding a trap and a reverse to keep the defense honest. The scrubs worked with growing enthusiasm, running the plays hard, sounding off with peppy talk.

Scotty found his spirits rising. These boys were putting some pride into their thankless job. This was going to be fun—working with a unit, having an important task to perform. The dark thoughts that had haunted him after that Friday night episode began to fade into the background.

Even the paragraph in Pinley's column that night didn't worry him too much. Pinley had somehow found out about his run-in with Cowan in the dressing room. He'd made the most of it, finishing off with a lament that "a feud between those two could be disastrous to next year's team."

The item upset John Durham, but Scotty assured him the whole thing was exaggerated. Pressed for details, he made them sound as harmless as possible.

"This Cowan—he been giving you trouble?" his uncle asked.

"Oh, he's a pretty good guy," Scotty answered. "We'll get along okay."

He was glad Aunt Alice came into the room just then to interrupt the conversation. Aunt Alice, it turned out, had something on her mind. She proposed the idea of Scotty's giving a party in their home.

It caught Scotty by surprise. "Why—that'd be nice. Of course . . . well, I don't know many people very well—"

"I don't mean right away," she said. "I know you're very busy now, getting started in your school work. In

87

a month or so, perhaps. As for being acquainted, that would be one reason for our party—a chance to meet some new friends."

"Now, Alice," John Durham put in, "don't push the boy. He may not care much about parties. Kids these days have their own ways of getting acquainted."

Alice Durham smiled. "John, you know even less about youngsters than I do. All young folks like parties."

Scotty blurted, "I've been invited to one party already."

"Wonderful!" his aunt exclaimed. "Tell us about it."

Scotty flushed in confusion. He wished he'd kept quiet. He'd wanted to say something to please Aunt Alice, and he had spoken without thinking. But there was no backing down now.

"Joan Cantrell is giving a party at her ranch. Actually, I haven't really received the invitation yet, but a girl at school told me all the football boys would be asked."

"At the Cantrell ranch! You'll have a wonderful time, Scotty. They have a perfectly fabulous place."

"That's what Julie called it—fabulous."

"Julie?"

"Julie Fisher. A girl I happened to meet. She's a majorette and secretary of the Junior Class."

John Durham winked knowingly. "See, Alice, I told you he wouldn't have any trouble meeting the right people."

"She's just an acquaintance," Scotty said hastily.

His aunt Alice smiled. "Well, I think it's marvelous

88

you got to know her and are invited to the Cantrell's. We'll talk about our party later. . . . Come on, John, let's give him a chance to do his homework."

Scotty wished he hadn't mentioned that invitation— an invitation he hadn't even received yet!

Oh, well, he did have some homework. Plenty of it.

When Coach Foster called the scrubs into the first huddle next afternoon, he said, "Run a few other plays before you try the option play."

They tried two handoffs, a fullback counter. They were stopped for little or no gain every time. First stringers were hollering, "Come on, scrubs, we need some real practice!" . . . "When you gonna open up something?" . . . "We're not even getting up a good sweat!"

The taunts were all in good humor, but the scrubs felt the sting of them just the same.

"Now," Foster told them in the huddle.

The scrubs lined up eagerly. Scotty took the ball and faked to the right half. Now was the instant of decision —keep or pitch. McGraw was playing off the fullback's block, staying wide. Split vision told Scotty that Keegan at tackle had been frozen momentarily by the right half's fake.

Scotty took off. He had to sidestep a lunge by Keegan, and then he was through, eluding Cowan by a full step, skimming past Gaddis' diving tackle, cutting back sharply into an open field. Allred and Hodges closed in. Leighton hurried over. Scotty reversed his field, trying to shoot the gap between Hodges and Leighton. He almost made it. Then Leighton's hurtling tackle bounced him. He'd come twenty yards.

"That's the play!" Jeffers told his team. "The old keeper. Montclair uses it a lot, and their quarterback can really run." He huddled them to review defensive assignments.

After that it got tougher. The regulars knew Scotty was in there to run the keeper, and they were laying for him. Keegan hit him. Cowan hit him. Gaddis hit him. Or a pile of them. And when those fellows tackled you, you stayed tackled!

Cowan had been slamming in fast from his corner post. Scotty had an idea. In the huddle he whispered a message to his right end. When Cowan came crashing in, the end, using Cowan's own momentum, blocked him *in*. Scotty cut outside and sprinted. With a quick jump on the tertiary, he was loose and gone.

The scrub end grinned at Cowan. "Kinda foxed you, didn't we, big boy? A little medicine Clayburn and I cooked up."

Cowan glowered and said nothing.

"That was nice," Scotty told the end. "Perfect."

Moments later he was hit at the line by Keegan, and as he went down, Cowan dived, burying a knee in his side. Scotty lay there, gasping a moment, feeling a little sick.

Foster rushed over. "You hurt, son?" Obviously, none of the coaches had seen that deliberate knee.

"I'm okay." Scotty got up, filling his lungs with a gulp of fresh air. There was Cowan again, he was thinking. The guy couldn't bear to be shown up, even a little bit.

The second team came in, and they were nearly as tough as the first, and the scrubs were getting tired. But they kept the defense busy until Jeffers finally called a halt.

As they went in, McGraw said to Scotty, "Busy day, eh?"

Scotty returned the big wingman's grin. "Rugged."

"How you like that T quarterback, compared to the old tailback job?"

"Wouldn't be fair to say. I've still got so much to learn about the T."

Allred said, "Learns fast though, doesn't he, Red?"

"He gave me all the trouble I wanted on that option play," McGraw averred. "You know, Clayburn, you're going to be a pretty valuable man around here—impersonating the opposition star player every week."

"If I last that long," Scotty said with a laugh.

Others joined their group, swapping casual, friendly talk. It was the first time in a week, Scotty reflected, they had included him. It sure gave a fellow a different feeling.

It was turning out as he'd hoped. After that first shock from Pinley's column, they'd had time to think it over. And they were beginning to doubt those insinuations. Before long they would probably forget the whole thing.

In the next few days he also sensed a change among students outside of football. The cool manner he'd encountered among certain classmates began to thaw. He no longer felt the covert glances, the low-voiced comments he had noted the previous week. And Eddie

Skeen, who'd acted actually hostile, began to chin with him before and after geometry class. "I'm going to stick close to you in this class, Clayburn," he said with a grin. "You're a shark in this math. Me, I'm a dunce."

It was Friday when Julie stopped him in the hall to say, "Remember, I was telling you about Joan's party. The date is set now—two weeks from Saturday. Better mark your calendar. You'll probably receive an invitation in a few days."

"Are you sure, Julie? Joan hardly knows me."

Julie laughed. "Oh, she knows you, all right."

Whatever that meant, Scotty thought, it sounded good, and he felt relieved. He'd worried a little about telling Aunt Alice he was going to the party.

It would be nice to have a date with Julie for that night. But that was hoping for too much. Julie's dates, he'd learned, went to Fred Gaddis. Anyway, he was glad a lot of the fellows would be going without dates. Julie was the only girl he knew well enough to ask.

The squad took a bus to Montclair next morning and played that night. The game turned out to be another one-sided victory for Westland, 41–6.

It was obvious from newspaper accounts that it had been a big night for Rex Cowan. Against a defense set to slow the wide stuff, Westland had called on Cowan a lot, down the middle and off tackle. And the big boy had really turned in a performance—over 200 yards rushing and four touchdowns.

"The greatest one-man exhibition of power running we've seen in some years," the *Times* reported.

Curiously enough, it was the same *Times* sports section that carried a story on Scotty Clayburn. It was a simple, factual story which briefly reviewed Scotty's record at Mayville, mentioned that he'd come to Westland High for some vocational work not offered at his hometown school, and said that he'd been working out with the squad, was showing ability, and was a good prospect for next year's team.

John Durham was disappointed. "Carlton could have said a lot more than that," he grumbled.

Scotty was glad he hadn't. Very glad. And now, maybe this would be the last of the publicity on the newcomer from Mayville. He surely hoped so.

Chapter
Eleven

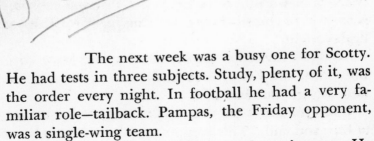

The next week was a busy one for Scotty. He had tests in three subjects. Study, plenty of it, was the order every night. In football he had a very familiar role—tailback. Pampas, the Friday opponent, was a single-wing team.

Rex Cowan did not take part in the scrimmage. He had received a cut on the cheekbone in some contact work the day before, and Jeffers thought it wise not to risk breaking the stitches.

As hero of the week, Cowan was carrying his fame rather gracefully, Scotty noted with agreeable surprise. After that performance at Montclair, one might expect Cowan to be strutting big this week. Instead, he was being almost modest about it. Maybe this was what the

94

guy needed. Now that he owned the glory spot without question, he was happy and content.

And he owned the spot, no doubt about it. "Never saw him run with so much power," Dave told Scotty. "Our stuff was working good, but Rex was getting those extra yards." And Hodges remarked, "He sure was barreling in there. If he keeps going like that, it's money in the bank. Nothing like a hard-running full-back to keep the defense honest."

The scrubs had trouble executing the single-wing blocking, but they gave the regulars a good workout. Scotty broke loose twice for big yardage and completed a few passes. As the defense jelled against the un-familiar formation, however, most of the scrub efforts ended under a pile of tacklers. But that was the pur-pose of it, of course—to get the team ready for Pampas Friday night.

At Bob's invitation, Scotty went to the game with Bob, Phil, and Esco. "Esco finally agreed to go if you were along," Bob had said.

When the teams came out to warm up, Scotty turned to Esco and said, "This Pampas team uses a single-wing formation. It operates off an unbalanced line; that is, four linemen on one side of center and two on the other."

"Uhuh," Esco grunted. "Strong point is concentra-tion of power at the point of attack. Weakness, plays to the weak side—unless you have a very fast wingback. Best defense is usually an overshifted six, with—"

"Wait a minute!" Scotty grimaced. "Has somebody been pulling my leg? I thought—"

"You thought I didn't know anything about football," Esco said without smiling. "Sorry you got that impression, but I don't believe I ever said that."

"Then, why—" Scotty broke off, a little warning clicking in his brain. Somehow he suddenly realized Esco didn't want to discuss the point further. What a puzzling guy!

As they watched the game, there were two things that marred the pleasure of the evening a little for Scotty.

One was the fact that Westland's team was having an off night and came mighty close to losing.

The other thing was some hecklers seated behind Scotty's group who kept up a running fire of loud-mouthed comments on the "lousy" play of the home team. They were insultingly personal in their comments on the players. Scotty found it very irritating.

But there were pleasant aspects to the evening too. For one, the halftime show by the band and drill team, a spectacle Scotty was seeing for the first time. The truth was, however, he kept his eye on one point of the show most of the time—the honey-blond majorette, second from left.

Then, best of all, Westland rallied to win the game. It was a narrow squeak, but in the final period Cowan's power into the line sparked a drive that gave them the tying touchdown, and Leighton's kick for point put them ahead 21–20.

As they left the stadium, Esco said to Scotty, "Being in the crowd gives you a different viewpoint, doesn't it?"

"What? Oh, you mean those loudmouths. Not many

people in the stands like those creeps, I imagine."

"There's a lot more of them than you think," Esco said.

Scotty didn't argue the point. There was a bitterness in Esco's tone, and Scotty was sure of one thing now—there was something behind that bitterness. Someday he was going to find out what it was.

The next week Scotty returned to his T halfback post. Rockview, the next opponent, used a flanker most of the time, a fast man to get down on passes—and to help weaken the middle defense. Scotty was playing the flanker spot.

On the first few plays he did decoy duty. Then they began to use the passes. Three times Scotty cut in behind Cowan to take short throws. Jeffers wasn't happy about it. "That flanker is your man, Cowan. Stay with him!"

Cowan didn't seem happy either. But he didn't say anything.

In the scrub huddle Foster said, "Let's cross them up. The fullback power play."

On this one Scotty had a tough assignment—to block the corner backer as the fullback came off tackle. He inched in a little to get a better blocking angle. When the ball was snapped, he feinted a movement downfield, then swerved to throw a body block into Cowan. Rex tried to get a hand under Scotty and pitch him off, but Scotty's hip snapped against Cowan's thigh, pinning him as the fullback went by with the ball.

Scotty kept digging to maintain contact. Then something like a cleaver came down on his neck, chopping him to the ground. He lay there, dazed a moment. He knew what had happened. Cowan had whacked him with the side of his hand, a gross infraction of the rules.

Scotty's first reaction was surprise. He'd had no clash with Cowan recently and expected none. Cowan, basking in the light of star performer the past two weeks, had seemed an almost different person—cooperating on the field, mixing in the friendly exchange of the locker room.

After surprise came anger. What Cowan had done was more than illegal. It was dangerous. A player could be seriously hurt that way.

Scotty got up and looked at Cowan. "Don't ever do that to me again," he said softly.

He wanted no trouble with Cowan. But he'd taken a lot off the guy, one way and another, and it was getting a little tiresome.

Four plays later it happened again. Cowan crouched, trying to fend off the block, but Scotty's charge was too quick. He slammed a hip into Cowan's midriff—and the hand came bludgeoning into his neck, almost stunning him senseless for a moment. Dimly, he was aware that Cowan had now escaped the block and was in swift pursuit of the runner to aid in the tackle.

Scotty got up, fury in his eyes. He was mad clean through. It wasn't just the physical pain; it was the deliberate dirtiness of the thing. He walked up to Cowan. "I'm warning you, Cowan. You do that once more, and I'll let you have it with both fists."

Cowan seemed to think it was amusing. "You guys

hear that?" He laughed. "He's threatening me."

Players nearby were looking at them curiously. They saw Cowan's smirking grin, Scotty's white-lipped anger. By strange coincidence, the coaches, who were conferring for a moment, missed the entire thing.

A few minutes later Jeffers said, "One more play, and the second unit will take the defense."

That was the irony of it. One more play. Later, Scotty was to think many times—if only Foster hadn't called that *certain* play.

But he did call it. So they ran it—fullback power play.

Cowan must have smelled it coming. He charged in, arms extended, bent on making the tackle at the line of scrimmage. Scotty drove toward him, head on. There wasn't much time. It would have to be a running shoulder block.

He hit Cowan. He hit him with a savage fierceness born of all the anger pent inside him. The impact was terrific. Cowan went down like a felled steer, and Scotty, riding the momentum of his own drive, crashed down on him.

Scotty picked himself up. Cowan rose to a sitting position, then lay back down with a groan.

Jeffers was there quickly, bending over Cowan. "Get the wind knocked out of you, son?"

"I . . . I'm hurt," Cowan gasped. His voice hardened. "He kneed me in the ribs, the dirty little—"

"Here, none of that!" Jeffers went down on one knee. "Where does it hurt?"

Cowan pointed to his left side. "He kneed me deliberately, after I was down—"

"Take it easy," Jeffers said. "Whatever happened was an accident."

"It was no accident! He was sore because I got away from his block a while ago. He threatened me. Ask Beddo or Dupre. They heard him—"

"Cowan!" Jeffers' voice was steel sharp. "Okay, men, step back. You two, help him to his feet. Careful!"

He pulled up Cowan's jersey and examined a red welt just above the blocking pad. He dropped the jersey and said to Jim Boone, "Better take him down to the clinic for an X ray."

He turned, and Scotty was standing there, white-faced.

"It could have been a knee—when we fell . . . I'm sorry—"

"I know, son. Those things happen. . . . All right, everybody, back to your places. Second unit in here on defense."

An hour later the report came to them in the dressing room. The X ray had told the story. Cowan had a broken rib. He would be out of action for at least three weeks.

There was an agitated murmur, then glum silence as the news spread over the room. As he finished dressing, Scotty could feel eyes turning toward him. He wanted to say something—to tell them how much he regretted this. But he didn't know where to start.

Then Del Keegan broke the long silence. "Well, there goes half of our backfield strength for the next three games."

Dave Franklin said, "It's a tough break. And I'm sure Scotty is just as sorry as anybody it happened."

"He's sorry now maybe," Harry Dupre said. "But, brother, he sure went in there bent on giving Cowan the works. I was pulling back and saw the play. I never saw a guy hit with a block like Clayburn put on Cowan."

Red McGraw said, "That was his assignment, wasn't it?"

"To block him, yeh," Chuck Beddo put in. "But not to cripple him."

Scotty stepped out in front of Beddo. "Let's get one thing straight," he said tautly. "I didn't knee Cowan purposely."

Beddo, standing a head taller than Scotty, looked at him a moment, then shrugged. "Okay, maybe I was out of line with that crack. But Cowan sure wasn't lying when he said you threatened him. I saw you barreling up to him—"

Dave came to Scotty's defense. "Let's be reasonable about this. If Scotty threatened Rex, he must have had some reason."

"Does it matter?" Keegan smiled bitterly. "Being sore at a guy is no excuse for personal revenge on the practice field."

"Just the same," Dave persisted, "Cowan must have done something to him. Is that right, Scotty?"

Scotty had his chance then. Dave was trying to help, to open the way for some sort of explanation. But all at once a cold bitterness welled up in him. He was tired of having to explain things, deny things, justify him-

101

self. Ever since he'd been here, he'd been explaining things to people. He was through explaining. He was fed up.

He spoke, his voice flat and hard. "Like Keegan said, what does it matter? You'll believe what you want to believe anyway." He turned and walked out the door.

Dave started after him, then stopped. He looked around at the others. "I think we're making a mistake. Scotty is not the kind to deliberately injure somebody."

Dupre said, "You didn't see his eyes when he walked up to Cowan out there. Boy, I wouldn't want anybody to look at me like that!"

Then Keegan asked, "How do we know so much about Clayburn? He *seems* okay, yes. But how long have we known him? About three weeks. You don't learn everything about a guy in three weeks."

McGraw spoke up. "So we don't know everything. So let's be fair and give him the benefit of the doubt."

"I don't know," Beddo said. "You know something? I'm still not sure that rich uncle of his didn't pay him to come here."

"Aw, come on, Beddo," McGraw said sharply. "Don't get off on that again."

"You suspected it yourself," Beddo retorted. "I heard you, coming in from the field the first day—"

"Maybe I've changed my mind." McGraw turned and went back to his locker.

Dave looked around uncertainly and said nothing. Seeing their faces, he knew that words right now would be of no avail.

Chapter
Twelve

The bad news was all over school by noon next day.

And talk flew thick and fast. Scotty could hear snatches of it: "A broken rib? Oh, no! Why, he's our best player." . . . "He practically won the last two games single-handed." . . . "Be out three games? Boy, that's rough." . . . "How'd it happen?" . . . "The way I hear it, this Clayburn guy—that transfer—got sore at him and gave him the business."

There was more of it—talk Scotty couldn't hear. But he could see the tight little groups conversing in low tones, the quick glances as he passed. And he knew pretty well what they were saying: Clayburn had threatened to get Cowan and he'd got him. He'd thrown a knee into Cowan when he was down. Who is this Clayburn? You know, the guy somebody found in a little burg and brought in here to play football.

In the locker room there was no more talk. Only cool, hostile silence. But Scotty could sense their thoughts: Maybe Cowan wasn't the most popular guy on the squad. Maybe he'd been pretty cocky at times. But he wasn't such a bad guy either. His attitude had improved a lot lately, hadn't it? And he was valuable to the team. They needed him. Now they'd lost him for three games, maybe four—all because Clayburn got sore at him. Yeh, maybe Cowan hadn't been too friendly toward Clayburn, but that was no reason for Clayburn to give him a knee out there. That was no way to settle a grudge.

Okay, let them think what they wanted to. Sure, it would be simple to tell them the whole thing: Cowan had been hacking him on the neck and he'd told Cowan to lay off or he'd sock him. As for the knee, he was blocking the guy, that's all. The knee—if it had been a knee—was purely accidental. Hadn't they ever seen a guy hurt in football before?

Yes, he could tell them. But what good would it do? If a person believed in you, you didn't have to explain. If he didn't believe in you, he wouldn't believe your explanation either.

Besides, he was tired of explaining. Let Cowan explain. Let Cowan tell what really happened. Only Cowan wasn't going to tell anything. Cowan was going to wait for *him* to explain—then deny the whole thing. Because Cowan was sure by now that nobody had seen him hit Scotty. There was no witness to support Scotty. So if it came to that, Cowan would bluff it out and say Scotty was lying to cover up his bad temper and dirty play.

Dave Franklin's voice broke in on his thoughts. "Boy, you are in a deep study. I've called your name three times."

Scotty looked up. "Yeh, I was thinking, I guess."

Dave said, "Look, Scotty, try not to worry about it. The fellows feel pretty glum about losing Cowan. They'll get over it and feel different."

"Maybe so." Scotty didn't want to talk about it.

"It might help, Scotty, if you'd tell them you're sorry you lost your temper—and also tell them why you were mad."

Scotty sat up straight. "So I lost my temper. Look, my assignment was to block the guy. I blocked him. Do I have to lose my temper to do that?"

Dave shook his head slowly. "Scotty, you don't know how hard you hit him. I saw the play, too."

Scotty said coldly, "It seems everybody saw *that* play. I go into Cowan with a shoulder block. Would I pick that way to hurt a man who outweighed me forty pounds?"

"That's what I'm saying. You didn't intend to hurt him. But when you get so mad you hate a guy, you can do something you didn't intend to."

"You mean—yeh, I guess that's how it was," Scotty

finished in a lifeless tone. He got up and started for the door.

"Listen, Scotty, I think you misunderstood what—"

"Forget it!" The words leaped out, sharp as steel darts. Scotty walked out, leaving Dave standing there.

Outside, his pace slowed. Something was telling him to go back, to tell Dave he was sorry he'd flared in anger. But something that was stronger—a hurt, stubborn pride—wouldn't let him do it. He kept going, on out to the field.

In the dark mood that had been upon him, he had not reckoned with the probability that Jeffers would question him about the incident. But when Chigger Rambo told him after the workout that Jeffers wanted to see him, Scotty was not surprised.

Now he was in Jeffers' office, facing the problem: How much was he going to tell the coach?

Lee Jeffers came straight to the point. "Rex says you threatened him. What did you say that he calls a threat?"

"I told him to lay off or I'd sock him with both fists."

"You made no threat to 'get' him, implying you would try to put him out of action?"

"No, sir, I did not."

"Now," Jeffers' eyes narrowed, "you said you'd hit him if he didn't lay off *what?*"

Scotty said, "I'd rather he told you that, sir."

Jeffers studied Scotty's face, noting the stubborn set of the jaw. "Mr. Kenwood is distressed by this incident. He fears bad publicity, especially from Pinley. Now I need to know both sides of this thing. I have to know what Cowan did that made you angry. He says he doesn't know. Apparently nobody saw anything. If I'm to find out, you'll have to tell me."

Scotty had already gone over it in his mind many times. Suppose he told the coach what Cowan had done—one of the dirtiest tricks a man could pull. Cowan would deny it. It would be his word against Cowan's. Jeffers would have to make a choice. If he chose to believe Scotty, Cowan would be in for a severe reprimand, possibly suspension. That would make Jeffers the target of some bitter criticism. He'd be putting himself on Scotty's side against one of his regular players—a player who was now the team star and a hero all over town.

No, Scotty decided. The coach had gone out on a limb far enough already "defending" him.

So he said, "I thought he was trying to dirty me. I could have been mistaken. I can't be positively sure, so I don't want to say."

Jeffers eyed him gravely. "And that is all you have to say?"

"Yes, sir. Except one thing. Whatever I did to break his rib was not intentional."

"If I thought it was intentional, you'd be suspended from the squad already." Jeffers sighed heavily. "I hope you realize this is going to make things bad for you— not clearing up the facts. Mr. Kenwood may even ask you to turn in your suit."

Scotty winced at that but remained stubbornly silent.

Jeffers said, "All right, you may go."

The bad publicity arrived on schedule. John Durham came into Scotty's room that night, tossing a copy of the *Express* on the desk. "That Pinley again! Read it!"

Scotty didn't want to read it. He'd had about enough for one day. But he picked up the paper and read the first paragraph.

Bad blood between two Westland football players (reported exclusively in the *Express* last week) reached the explosion point on the field yesterday. And when the smoke of battle cleared, one of the kids was on his way to the hospital. And, believe it or not, the loser in the rock-and-sock climax to this feud was not the spidery little halfback from Mayville. No, sir, it was the big and rugged fullback, Rex Cowan.

Scotty skimmed over the rest of it. It was about what he'd expected. Details exaggerated. A few extra ones invented. And just enough truth to give the worst possible impression.

His uncle fumed, "Compare that with the way the *Times* handled it. Just said the boy received a rib fracture in scrimmage. Didn't even name you. Carlton's decent enough to know those things happen in football and nobody is to blame. By the way, what does Jeffers think about it?"

Scotty framed his answer very carefully. He didn't want his uncle going to the coach. "He's been real nice. He knows it was just an accident."

"I'd like to wring that Pinley's neck!" John Durham growled. Then he smiled wryly. "But the best thing is to ignore it. If anybody brings it up, I'm going to say it's some more of Pinley's lies and drop the subject. Less said now, the better."

On that point, Scotty reflected with relief, he and his uncle agreed exactly.

But Pinley's story was not the last of the "bad press" for Scotty. In the *Zephyr*, which was issued on Friday morning, Eddie Skeen had inserted a "late lead" over the main story on the sports page in which he played up Cowan's injury and loss to the team. Then Skeen had added a loaded sentence: "Oddly enough, it was 146-pound Scotty Clayburn, the transfer from Mayville, whose crushing block sidelined the 187-pound Cowan."

The readers could draw their own conclusions from that!

As Scotty's eye roamed absently over the rest of the paper, he stopped suddenly on a little item: "Invitations have been received by nearly a hundred students to the barbecue and dance to be held Saturday evening at the ranch home of Joan Cantrell. . . ."

He read no more. Clayburn hadn't received any, that was for sure.

Thinking it all over, Scotty knew there was something he must do. He must talk to Rex Cowan. It would likely prove a futile thing, but he had to make the try anyway. Cowan was back in school, he knew. Perhaps he'd see the fullback today.

The opportunity came sooner than he expected. As he left the lunchroom, there was Cowan getting a drink at the water fountain. They were alone for the moment.

Scotty said, as pleasantly as he could, "How's the rib? Getting along okay?"

Cowan regarded him sourly. "I was lucky it didn't puncture a lung."

That, Scotty knew, wasn't true. It hadn't even been that type of fracture. But he only said, "I'm sorry it happened. It sure wasn't intentional."

"Yeh?" Cowan sneered. "I'll bet it wasn't!"

Scotty saw it was no use. His mouth tightened. "You're not going to tell them you deliberately hacked me on the neck, are you?"

"What are you talking about, Clayburn? I was trying to fight off a block. I've got a right to use my hands. If a hand slipped and hit you on the neck, so what? What're you beefing about anyway? Who got the busted rib in this deal?"

"Okay, Cowan." Scotty smiled coldly. "But *you* know and *I* know—don't we." He stood there long enough to see Cowan's red face lose some of its color. Then he walked away.

A tired, discouraged feeling weighed down on him as he went to his hall locker at the end of the sixth period. It had been a depressing day.

"Scotty."

He turned. It was Julie Fisher.

"Glad I saw you," she said. "There's something I wanted to say."

Scotty wasn't too glad, but he tried to sound agreeable. "Here I am, with time on my hands. No workout today, so I'm on my way home as soon as I get some books." The team had left for Rockview.

"Then we both have time to talk," she said. "This is tennis period and I can be a little late."

"You practice in the fall too?" He'd heard she was number one on the girls' team.

"We practice the year round, weather permitting. And the weather has to be pretty rough before our coach calls off a workout."

There was an awkward pause. Then she said, "I saw Joan's list of guests . . . I'm sorry, Scotty."

"It's okay." He shrugged. "I'm snowed under with homework this weekend anyway."

Her blue eyes clouded. "I don't know how to apologize, Scotty—for talking too much and building you up for a letdown. First, the speech. Then this. I feel pretty horrible about it."

"It's not your fault, Julie. Forget it." Any other time he would have been more concerned over Julie's embarrassment than his own. But the mood he was in today, what he felt most was a kind of irritation about it all.

"Scotty"—she hesitated a long interval before going on—"I heard about the accident on the field. Fred said you were awfully sore at Rex. You didn't intend to hurt him, did you?"

"No—and I'd rather not talk about it." So Fred had told her. She would get her information from Fred Gaddis, of course.

She looked at him. "Tell me, Scotty. What did Rex do that made you so angry at him?"

Scotty stiffened. So that was it. They wanted to per-suade him to talk. And Gaddis had sent Julie around to do the job. Julie, they figured, would be quite per-suasive. Well, it wouldn't work. He wasn't giving them a chance to say he'd "made up a crazy alibi" as an after-thought.

He answered, a little sharply, "I said I didn't want to discuss it."

She shook her head in mild exasperation. "Don't you realize your stubborn pride is making it harder for you? You won't talk, and so the boys think you really have nothing to tell—no excuse to justify yourself. Can't you see that?"

Irritation crept into Scotty's voice. "Look, Julie, you're butting in on something here that doesn't con-cern you. Now, if you don't mind, let's drop the subject."

A quick flush flooded her face. "I suppose you're right. It doesn't concern me. And you can be sure I won't bother you about it again. Good-by, Scotty." She was gone, her rapid steps echoing down the hall.

Scotty stood there feeling completely miserable. What had come over him? He'd had no cause to talk that way to Julie. Nobody around here had been any nicer to him than Julie. Maybe she was their mes-senger, but he'd bet she didn't really know what was behind their scheme. She'd been interested only in helping him.

Well, she wouldn't be interested anymore. There had been a very final sound to that "good-by."

Chapter
Thirteen

Many times during that weekend Scotty went over in his mind what he would say to Coach Jeffers on Monday. His presence on the squad from the start had caused misunderstanding and trouble—trouble for the coach, for the school. It would be best for him to turn in his suit.

He told himself many times that his mind was made up, that it was the thing to do. But each time some inner voice told him he would never do it. *Use all the fancy words and reasons you want to, Clayburn, but they'll still add up to just one word—quitter.*

So on Monday morning he was aboard an early bus to arrive in time for "skull" practice. The coach would likely have a busy session this morning, pointing out the mistakes made down at Rockview. Westland had won 28–15 but from all reports had played spotty ball. No doubt they'd missed the services of Rex Cowan.

As he stepped off the bus he heard "Hey, Scotty."

He looked around. It was Bob, Phil, and Esco, and two other boys from the radio class.

"What are you guys doing up here this early?"

Bob said, "We figured you'd be on this bus. We want to talk over something with you. Got a few minutes?"

"Sure," Scotty said. "I'm a little early."

"You know we talked about organizing an Electronics Club," Bob said. "Well—Scotty, we want you to be our president."

For a moment Scotty was speechless. Then he said, "Hey, wait a minute. Is this the way you elect a president? I thought it was done by a popular vote of the club."

"Yeh," Bob said, "but we've talked to everybody that's joining up. They want you. It's practically unanimous. Only thing, we wanted to check with you, make sure you'd accept."

"Come to think of it, I can't. Meetings will be right after school, won't they?"

"Mostly, yes."

"And I'll be tied up with football."

"We thought about that," Bob said. "We'll meet on Friday. You're off on some Fridays."

"Not all of them," Scotty said. "It wouldn't be fair to the club. I wouldn't have time to do justice to the job."

114

Phil said, "We want you anyway. The vice president can fill in till after football season. Then you can take over."

"Well," Bob said, "what do you say, Scotty?"

Scotty wished he could say what he really felt. This was their way of telling him they were still for him. This was their answer to the slurs they'd been hearing. They were showing where they stood by offering him a special honor.

He could never put into words the gratitude he felt. He just said, "I appreciate this an awful lot. But a president—well, he should be able to give a lot of time to club activities. I can't do it now. So I'm going to have to say no."

"You wouldn't like to think it over awhile?" one of the other boys said.

Scotty shook his head. "Get somebody who can really be on the job. You've got a lot of good fellows to pick from."

"Gosh, I'm sorry, Scotty." Bob sighed. Then his old grin came back. "You're too darned conscientious."

"If you ask me," Esco said, "he's just hardheaded."

Scotty grinned. "Esco, you hit the nail with your head."

It was good to feel like smiling again.

In football, though, he found little to smile about. As the days passed into weeks, he began to realize that something had happened to his performance out there. He carried out his role—the position of the opposition key back each week—but somehow much of the old thrill of the game was gone.

Among the players, time was softening the resentment caused by the Cowan incident. Some of them swapped talk with him, not especially friendly, but not hostile. Red McGraw was even friendly, in his detached and impersonal manner. But the barrier was still there, an invisible thing that set him apart.

Even with Dave. His and Dave's conversation around the lockers was pleasant enough. But something was missing from their old friendship. The warmth was gone. Far back in Scotty's mind was the nagging knowledge that he was largely at fault for this. But he could not bring himself to face it openly and make the first move.

On the field there were no incidents. They tackled him hard in scrimmage, but it was clean, impersonal, all a part of the day's work. Cowan, who was not yet ready to resume contact work, ignored him studiedly, never speaking at all.

Jeffers had had no further conference with him. Nothing had come of the fear that Mr. Kenwood might ask Scotty to drop out of football. Maybe Jeffers had talked him out of it; Scotty never knew. The head coach had plenty of other things to claim his attention. They were wading through the district schedule, and every game was important. They had little trouble beating San Palo 26–6, but Kimball gave them a scare before the Tigers finally eked out a 14–8 win. Cowan was still out, but was due to return to the lineup in the next game.

Pinley, Scotty noted with some relief, seemed to have forgotten him. Pinley was finding more exciting topics for his daily gossip column. Clayburn was no longer a hot topic.

There was one person in the locker room who hadn't changed, whose loyalty to Scotty had never wavered—Chigger Rambo. And the little manager happened to be the one who passed on to Scotty some startling news. Oddly enough, however, it wasn't in the locker room, where they saw each other every day. It was at the all-school Harvest Dance in the gymnasium.

Scotty probably wouldn't have been at the dance if it hadn't been for Aunt Alice. Of course she'd read in the society pages about Joan Cantrell's party and doubtless had wondered what happened to Scotty's invitation. Too tactful to question him about it, she had done what she thought best to help him forget the snub—she'd reminded him it was about time they started planning his party.

Scotty wished she would forget it. He didn't want a party, not the elaborate social affair she had in mind. But he couldn't tell her that. He tried to hedge, pleading too much schoolwork. But she insisted he needed fun and relaxation along with work.

Then, desperately searching for an out, he had mentioned the all-school dance. "I plan to attend that, Aunt Alice, and that's about all the partying I have time for now."

"All right," she'd said, plainly disappointed. "But promise me you'll go to that."

Having gone that far, he had to follow through. Getting a date for the dance was simpler than he'd expected. He remembered Francine Clark, a girl who sat just in front of him in English. Francine was a nice, friendly sort, in a quiet way, and she just might accept. She did, without hesitation.

So he was here tonight with Francine. And as the couples promenaded into the gym for the first dance, Scotty saw Julie Fisher up ahead and Fred Gaddis— but they were not together. Julie was with Jim Harte. The girl on Fred's arm was a stranger to Scotty. It started him wondering.

Later, when someone cut in on him, he strolled over to a group of boys standing in a corner of the gym, and there he saw Chigger Rambo.

Chigger grinned. "Don't tell me you're stagging too."

"Nope," Scotty said. "Just resting this one out." Then he added, "I see Fred's not dating his regular girl tonight."

Chigger raised an eyebrow. "Didn't you know he and Julie had busted up?"

Scotty felt a little shock pass through him. "It's news to me."

Chigger said, "You didn't know Julie and Fred had a fuss over you?"

"Over me!" Scotty stared at him. "You're kidding."

Chigger gave him a strange look. "You really didn't know, did you? . . . Julie told Fred she didn't think you ought to be blamed for Cowan's injury, and she thought, him being the captain, Fred ought to take the lead in getting at the bottom of the thing—kind of clear it up with the team. Fred didn't agree and—well, you know, one argument led to another and"—Chigger shrugged—"well, I don't know all the details, but that's the gist of it."

Scotty said nothing. He was thinking, trying to grasp the whole meaning of what Chigger had disclosed to him. Then he heard the little fellow saying, "Is that your date, that girl trying to catch your eye? I think that jerk she's dancing with is stepping on her toes."

"Huh? Oh, thanks." Scotty tried to shake off his daze as he walked over and tapped the boy on the shoulder.

As they resumed dancing, Francine smiled and said, "Thanks, Scotty. That boy seemed to have four feet, all size twelve."

"Sorry," Scotty said. "Course, I'm no Fred Astaire myself."

"You're a very nice dancer," Francine said.

She was really a nice kid, Scotty thought. Pretty, too. But he found his mind wandering away from Francine far too much as the evening progressed. He kept remembering what Chigger had told him, remembering his last conversation with Julie and how it had ended. The more he thought about it, the surer he was that he had to talk to her. Just what he would say he wasn't sure, but he had to say something.

He got his chance, finally, to cut in. Julie's eyes seemed distant and impersonal as she and Scotty took up the lazy rhythm the band was playing at that moment. Scotty opened his mouth, then closed it. His brain felt numb. At last he managed to speak. "The Council really puts on a nice dance."

"Good music," Julie said. "Best combo we've had this year."

He'd have to do better than that. Maybe he should ask if he could see her sometime, that he had something he wanted to say to her.

The music stopped. A voice came over the loudspeaker: "Intermission, everybody. After you've had some refreshments, we'll present a floor show—"

Julie gave him a coolly polite smile and was gone.

After that it was a long evening. Scotty did his best to make it a pleasant one for Francine. But he was afraid he didn't succeed very well.

As the weeks went by, Scotty did his daily stint on the football field, but it wasn't much fun any more. Try as he did, he couldn't seem to recapture the old zest for it. More and more he concentrated on his class work—particularly radio, which he found more fascinating every day. He was the first to finish building a one-tube receiver and started well ahead of schedule on the schematic design for his superhet.

In his radio class, too, he had friends who accepted him without reservation. Day by day his association with Bob and Phil and Esco became closer. He visited in their homes. They came over to visit in his uncle's home.

But their favorite meeting place was Esco's workshop. Out behind the Hammers' brick house, Esco had a shop that contained everything to delight a tinkerer's heart. Scattered on a long worktable were tools, solder gun, wires, meters, old radio sets, and a hundred other odds and ends.

It was a Saturday night two weeks after the dance

that Scotty went over to work with Esco on a transistor set. After they'd worked about an hour, Esco said, "Let's take a break." He motioned Scotty to a chair. "What did you think of the game last night? Analyze it for me."

Scotty was accustomed by now to Esco's abrupt changes of topic, his unexpected questions.

They'd seen the game at Tiger Stadium. Still-unbeaten Westland had defeated a supposedly dangerous Calden team 21–0. "Defense mainly," Scotty said. "The line play was the difference. Keegan, Beddo, Dupre, Gaddis—they really closed the door on Calden's middle stuff and forced them to go outside, and they didn't have the speed for that."

Esco nodded. "That's the way I had it figured. The way we stopped their passing too. Concentrating on receivers, only three men rushing the quarterback. He wasn't a running threat."

On a sudden impulse Scotty said, "Esco, I can't figure you out. You know football and you seem to enjoy watching it—when you do go to a game. Yet you are, well, sort of anti-football. What's the angle?"

"I've got nothing against the game itself," Esco said. "It's the people who've ruined the game that I'm against."

"Ruined the game? Who says it's ruined? I don't get it."

Esco was silent a moment. "Look, I'm going to tell you something I've never told anyone in this town. You thought I was an only child, didn't you? Well, I

121

have an older brother—a seven-year gap between us. He lives in California, where we all lived till two years ago.

"You'll find this hard to believe, Scotty, but my brother Jeff was an athlete. A great one—big and beautifully built. I was thirteen when he was playing fullback on a junior college team in our hometown. You can imagine what a hero he was to me. Everybody said he was the most valuable player on the team. He loved the game and he played it hard.

"In the next to last game of the season he injured a knee. Not very seriously. It would have healed okay. Except that big last game was coming up, the game they *had* to win. And the coach put him in that game. Jeff rehurt the knee. And it was bad this time—really torn up. He had two operations, but they didn't help much. He's still got a bum knee he'll carry with him the rest of his life."

"Gee, that *is* tough," Scotty said.

"That's not all," Esco said. "Here's the tough part. His big dream was to get into the U.S. Air Force Academy. He'd already been nominated as an entrant. All he had to do was pass mental and physical tests. Of course he had to forget it. He couldn't pass any physical with that knee."

Scotty said, "I get your point. The coach did wrong putting him in there. But I don't believe there are many coaches who would do a thing like that."

"No, you don't get my point. *Why* did the coach do it? Because he'd lose his job if he didn't win. That's who I blame—the people who use their power to tell a coach he's got to win or get out. With them, football is not a game—it's a promotion. It's not run for the guys who play the game. It's all for the mob in the stands."

Scotty felt uncomfortable. Esco had been hit close to home where it really hurt. He was pretty bitter about it. Scotty didn't want to argue with him, but he said, "I know what you mean, Esco, but I don't think it's that way everywhere—"

"All right," Esco broke in, "take it right here in Westland. The kids get all steamed up like it would be a world tragedy if we lost a ball game—"

"There's nothing wrong with that, Esco. That's just good old school spirit."

"Okay, maybe the kids take it as good sports after it's all over. But not the grownups. You watch it. If Jeffers doesn't win state this year, they'll start grumbling. And if he doesn't get it next year—brother, he's had it in this town!"

Scotty smiled. "Now you *are* exaggerating, Esco."

But he had an uneasy feeling that Esco might be right. What he had said was awfully close, Scotty recalled, to what Uncle John had said back in September.

Scotty had seen Julie now and then around school, but he still hadn't spoken to her about the big thing that was on his mind. She was politely pleasant, no more. Against her cool reserve, he could not seem to summon the right words or the courage until the brief opportunity had passed.

Then one day he made up his mind. It was Friday. The team had left for a game at Dorado, and he was free the seventh period. Julie would be on the tennis courts, he hoped. It was a chilly afternoon, but bright and clear, and the tennis squad would likely be working out.

They were. Julie was warming up with another girl on the nearest of a battery of four courts. He waited and watched, admiring her proficiency with the racket. The girls played a practice set. Finally, Julie finished off set point with a deep forehand drive and came to the sideline.

Scotty said, "You play a fast game. Anybody in state that can beat you next spring?"

"Plenty of them." Julie smiled, toweling her face. She was perspiring freely, even in the chill November air. "I'm afraid I won't get through district if I don't sharpen up that backhand."

Scotty took a deep breath. "There's something I've wanted to say a long time, Julie. About the way I acted that day . . . well, you know the time I mean. I've been sorry about it ever since. I don't know how I could have been so rude—to you, especially."

"Forget that part of it, Scotty." She looked straight into his eyes. "Have you decided to answer the question I asked you that day?"

Scotty blinked. He hadn't expected that. "I'm sorry, Julie. I can't do that."

She smiled wanly. "Then nothing has really changed, has it, Scotty?" She picked up her spare racket. "Sorry to run. Coach doesn't like us to stand in the cool wind after exercise."

He watched glumly as she jogged toward the girls'

gym. Yes, he supposed she was right. Nothing had really changed. . . .

The Tigers kept winning. They beat Dorado 22–8, routed Kingston 41–14, and they were district champs. The bidistrict playoff against Burk City was tough, but they took it 13–0—and they were in the state semifinal against Concho.

It was a tossup, dopesters said. Westland's methodical power against Concho's brilliant wide-open play. The game was played at Concho, some ninety miles to the southeast, a booming oil town in the one-time sheep country. Westland went into the final quarter leading 14–13. Then four minutes before the gun, Concho uncorked a 50-yard pass and lateral play for the winning touchdown. A sad throng of rooters rode the buses and motor caravan back to Westland that night.

So the season was over. It had been a good one, eleven victories and one defeat. And when Concho beat Bayport 20–6 the next Saturday for the state championship, the students were consoled. At least they'd lost to the best team in the state.

But from the town came rumblings of complaint. Scotty got an echo of it from his uncle. "Folks are kind of disappointed," John Durham said. "Jeffers has been here five years and still hasn't had a state champion. I heard King Carruth say if he doesn't produce next year, it'll probably be his last."

Scotty could hold his silence no longer. "There's not a better coached team in the country than Westland. If they fire a man like Jeffers, they're crazy."

His uncle laughed. "Stick up for your coach, kid. Admire you for it. But you'll find that's how this town is. They don't like being *second* best."

Scotty wondered who "they" were. The people of the town as a whole? Or a few men who had ways and means of bringing pressure on the board and the administration? He hated to admit it, but it was beginning to look as if Esco might have been right after all.

"What are we worrying about?" his uncle was saying. "With you in that backfield next year, we'll win state, and everybody will be happy."

Scotty shook his head. "I hope it won't take all of that to make them happy. All the way to state is a long, tough road."

"Come now, Scotty, a little more confidence. Everybody is counting on you. You're the thing we've been needing here a long time. With you in there, we can't miss."

Scotty knew it was useless to argue the point, to try to make his uncle see how such talk put him on the spot.

And the worst of it was, he wasn't even sure he'd be a help to the team at all. He'd give it his best. He'd try. He'd snap out of that lassitude that had gripped him these past weeks. He'd made that vow to himself already.

But what about the others? Somehow, things had gone wrong and he'd failed to win their confidence. He was still an outsider who didn't quite belong. Would they be able to put aside personal feelings and play their best when he was in the lineup?

Only time, he supposed, would give the answer.

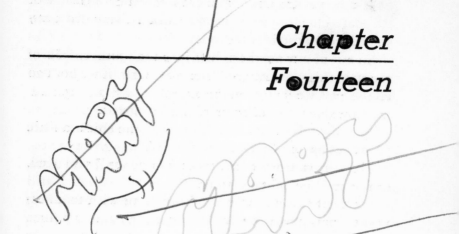

Chapter Fourteen

Red McGraw pulled on his jersey and said, "Have you guys seen that schedule Coach posted this morning? Know who we play in the second game?"

It was September again. In the dressing room the Westland squad was donning fresh, bright playing uniforms. This was the day, Jeffers had explained, the newspapers would be out to take pictures.

"Second game?" Scotty said. "Clearwater, isn't it?"

"Nope," McGraw said. "Concho."

"Concho!" Dave exclaimed. "How come?"

"One of those things," Red explained. "Clearwater canceled out. Concho had an open date the same week, and the two schools got together and scheduled it. Be played here. You can count on playing to a packed house that night, lads."

"Know what?" Dave said. "It might be a preview of the state championship game. Concho has been reassigned from District Five to District Seven. That moves them out of our northern half into the southern half of the state this year. After league play starts, if we both go all the way, we'll meet in the finals."

"Slow down there, podner," Red drawled.

"I know." Dave smiled. "Counting the chicks a little early. It was just an idea."

"Just in case we don't meet 'em again," said Red, "I'd sure like to take those babies this time. I still haven't got over the way they conned us with that last-minute pass play last year."

"They'll be tough," Dave said. "They have four ringers coming eligible this season." He added quickly, "Not classing you with those guys, Scotty. They're really 'recruited talent,' not just transfers."

"By the way, Scotty," said McGraw, "I hear your old coach at Mayville got fired after a bad season last year. Guess he didn't have much of a team without you."

"He had some good boys," Scotty said. "Just couldn't seem to get going, folks at home said."

He knew the real reason Kelley had been fired. His bad temper had finally tripped him. He'd completely lost control of the boys and the whole situation. Johnny Alderson had been promoted to head coach, which was a good turn of events for Mayville, Scotty figured.

McGraw said, "Boy, these new playing jerseys are pretty. Look at that bright red trim."

"Mine will probably stay pretty," Dave said. "I won't get in there enough to sweat it up good."

"Cheer up, pal." Red laughed. "It's some honor to be playing behind the two best halfbacks in the state."

Scotty felt a flush of embarrassment. Not that they intended their remarks as a barb at him. Dave and Red had been nothing but friendly ever since the opening of workout two weeks ago. He was very lucky to have his locker next to theirs.

But he felt bad that Dave still had not made the starting lineup. In spring practice Scotty had won a berth at left half. With Leighton and Allred graduated, he'd hoped Dave would be at the other halfback. But Jeffers had moved Cowan into that position. Hodges would be at quarterback again, of course, and stocky Cliff Burgamy, Cowan's understudy the year before, filled out the quartet at fullback.

So Dave was left out. And there was little doubt he would have been in one of the halfback slots if Scotty hadn't come along.

There'd been some talk about it, he knew—some resentment that Clayburn was shunting aside an old Westland boy who had worked hard two years for a place on the team. But it wasn't the talk that bothered Scotty. It was for Dave himself that he felt regrets. The way Dave had been cheerfully hiding his disappointment made it hurt.

"Well," McGraw said, "let's go get our pictures taken."

The man who took the pictures turned out to be a commercial photographer taking pictures for both papers. He shot the squad, then groups of backs and linemen, then began on individual action poses, getting one picture of each man among the top twenty-five. But when he got to Scotty, he said, "I have orders to get four or five of you."

Scotty didn't like it, but it would make him more conspicuous to argue with the man. So he said, "Okay, what will it be?"

The photographer took five shots: stance, plunging toward the camera, leaping for a pass, making a jump pass, cutting in an open field. When he had finished, Scotty walked back to where the squad was holding a light passing drill until the picture making was done.

And Cowan said, for everyone to hear, "For a guy who still hasn't played a down for this team, Clayburn sure rates with the press."

Some of the others kidded Scotty, too, but it was in good humor. It was Cowan's sour remark that troubled him. It was the first open show of hostility from him, and Scotty had hoped they could keep their personal differences submerged. But Cowan's weakness of jealousy was showing through again. One thing sure, if Cowan started creating friction between them, it could hurt the team and hurt it badly.

Apparently, the rest of them had decided to "go along" with the transfer from Mayville, although they still treated him with cool reserve. Only Dave and Red had shown any real cordiality. But in spring training and in the last two weeks, things had gone smoothly in practice. His teammates' attitude was pretty plain. Off the field, they would go their way and he could go his. But they respected his ability to play football, and on the field they would work with him.

It was a strange relationship. He wondered if the time would come when, under sudden stress, that relationship would crack and come apart.

They got back to real work that afternoon. Jeffers drove them hard, as he had done for the past two weeks. It had been a grind. Group drills, contact drills for blocking, ball carrying, tackling. Hitting the dummy, charging the sled. Signal drills, dummy scrimmage, full scrimmage. The bed had felt mighty good at night. But Scotty had enjoyed every minute of it. He was recapturing the old zest for the game he loved. And he had soaked up a wealth of football knowledge.

Physically, he was in prime condition. His uncle had got him a job for the summer as rodman with an oil-company surveying party. For ten weeks he had tramped over the dry plains, carrying rod and chain. And when the job was finished, Scotty was brown as a nut, his muscles hard as nails, and he had actually gained eight pounds.

At the dinner table that night John Durham said, "Watch that boy put away steak and potatoes, Alice."

"He's jealous, Scotty," Alice Durham laughed. "If he ate like that, he'd gain a pound a day."

"Guess I burn up a lot of fuel," Scotty said, grinning.

"That coach really works you kids, doesn't he?" his uncle said.

"Yes, sir. That's the way to build a ball club."

"Wouldn't argue with that. In fact, that's just what King Carruth was saying today. You know King. Met him last year, remember? By the way, he ran for school board last spring and was elected. Taking quite an interest in the team this year."

King Carruth. Scotty remembered him all right. Beetle brows. Gravelly voice. *Reminds me of the old days . . . we got 'em some ball players, didn't we?* So now he was on the school board. For some reason it gave Scotty an uneasy feeling.

"Looks like the greatest team in seven years," John Durham was saying. "That's the dope in the papers. Even from our cautious friend Carlton of the *Times*. With Clayburn to furnish the explosive punch, they're saying, Westland should cruise right down to the state final without getting up a heavy sweat."

"They" were starting early, Scotty thought. Building up hopes for a miracle team—and for a big letdown if the miracle team didn't materialize. He wished he could make his uncle see that.

On Monday the buildings of Westland High came to life with the invasion of three thousand boys and girls. Arranging classes, getting books and lockers issued, studying the first assignments—all these vied with football for Scotty's attention that week. He was enrolled in English, Solid Geometry, Economics, and Advanced Electronics.

Bob and Phil, who had taken radio as seniors, were gone, but Esco was back to join Scotty in electronics.

"Guess what I'm working on," Esco said, by way of greeting him.

"Sending signals to Mars?" Scotty suggested.

"A transceiver," Esco said, ignoring the joke. "I want you to build one too, and we can talk to each other. We're in easy range. We live less than a mile apart."

"A great idea, Esco. But I'm afraid I'll have to wait till after football season. Won't have much free time."

"Yeh, I guess so," Esco said in a tone of disappointment. "Say, this course is going to be something. Long-range broadcasting, radar, microwave. I can't wait to get into it."

"You and me both," Scotty said.

On Thursday Mr. Bechtel called Scotty out of study hall for a conference. "I wanted to have a little talk, Scotty," the teacher said. "First, tell me—what are your plans and ambitions?"

Scotty told him. When he finished, Mr. Bechtel said, "You have a sharp mind for this work, Scotty. Much too sharp to stop at merely being a repairman for radios and TV sets. You should go to college and study electronics. It's a great field, with no limit to the opportunities."

Scotty explained why he needed to start working and help with the family income.

"That's commendable of you," Mr. Bechtel said. "But I imagine it would make your mother very happy to see you go on and prepare yourself for something bigger. Think how much more you could do for her and yourself with college training. Now, as for the costs, there are scholarships, you know. I find you were an 'A' student not only in my work but also in

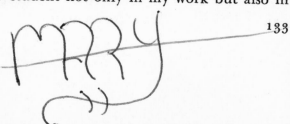

all other subjects. That's remarkably good, Scotty. And that's what scholarships are for—bright, energetic young people like you."

"I appreciate your interest, Mr. Bechtel," Scotty said. "But even if I could get a scholarship, there'd be some other expenses. And I couldn't help Mom during those four years. I'm afraid it's too much sacrifice for her to make."

"I see." The teacher nodded slowly. "Well, you don't have to decide today. But I do hope you'll give it some thought."

Scotty reflected a moment. It was an exciting thought—college and the big new world it would open up for him. But for him, he felt, it could never be more than a dream. "I'll think about it, sir." He got up to leave. "And thanks again."

"Oh, something else, Scotty."

"Yes, sir?"

Mr. Bechtel smiled. "I'm figuring to see you make at least two touchdowns against Brighton tomorrow night."

"Afraid I won't be that lucky." Scotty smiled back. "But come on out anyway. We'll try to make it interesting."

Friday brought the big welcoming and pep assembly. Just like last year, Scotty thought. Only this time he was seated in a reserved section up front with the football squad, and the yells seemed even louder, more spine tingling. And there was Dave, now president of the Student Council, up there on the stage, wearing a coat and tie and talking like an orator.

The majorettes came out and gave a baton-twirling act. Julie Fisher looked prettier than ever, Scotty thought. He wondered if he'd see much of Julie this year. Or if she'd be very interested in seeing him.

Now there was sudden quiet as Dave raised a hand, and three thousand voices joined in the Alma Mater. Then the great auditorium emptied as the band played the Tigers' Fight Song.

And Scotty was thinking: Ten hours from now—the kickoff. . . .

Most of that ten hours had passed now. The team had finished its warmup on the field and was back in the stadium dressing room, hearing Jeffers' final word before the game.

The coach called out the starting lineup. There were six new names in that lineup. In the backfield, Clayburn and Burgamy. On the line only McGraw, an end, and Dupre and Dent, guards, were back from last year. Tonight Jess Hollum was at the other end, Doug Ruthven and Tom McLarty at tackles, and Herb Brooks at center.

"We've never played this Brighton team before," the coach told them. "They come from over in East Texas, and as you know, our scout reports have been secondhand. But we do know they have a good, hard-blocking single-wing team, and that they didn't come three hundred miles out here for the ride. I believe you can beat them, but you'll have to block and tackle hard and drive hard—and stay mentally alert every minute. All right—let's go!"

They went down the ramp, right under the student section, and the yells poured down on them. Co-captains McGraw and Hodges met the officials and the Brighton captains out in the middle of the field. The coin went up; a Brighton captain called it wrong. Westland chose to receive. The starting lineup clamped on helmets. The squad bunched in a tight huddle for the traditional handclasp, then scattered—starters onto the field, others to the bench.

Scotty took his position a few steps in front of the goal line. On his right was Cowan, on his left Hodges. He flexed his knees, trying to relax the "kickoff jitters."

Brighton, in golden jerseys with blue numerals, lined up across field. Westland, jerseys white and numbers red, waited. The whistle blew; the golden line advanced. The kick. The ball soared, tumbling end over end—straight toward Scotty Clayburn.

His heart jumped. This was it. This was for real again—after a long time. His first game for Westland High.

Chapter
Fifteen

A lively breeze was carrying the kick deep. Scotty backed almost to the goal line, weighing his chances. He could play it safe, and the ball would easily roll past the end zone for an automatic touchback and be put in play on the 20-yard line.

He chose to run it out. And just as he reached for the ball, he heard Cowan's sharp yell: "Let it go!"

Scotty was strung pretty tight. After all, it was his first actual game in nearly two years. The yell was like a rasp on his taut nerves. He dropped the ball.

It rolled crazily to one side. He whirled around for it, reached—and his toe hit the ball, nudging it just over the goal line. He went after it. He could hear the soft thunder of Brighton cleats, coming ever closer. For a moment panic clawed at him.

Then his deep-seated football instinct took charge. He moved quickly, yet deliberately. Covering the ball now wasn't enough. He had furnished the impetus which sent it into the end zone. It would be a safety— and two points for Brighton.

He picked up the ball, spun around, and started back upfield. A tackler was bearing down on him. Scotty sidestepped the man, almost easily, and slanted left. A pack of golden jerseys was swarming toward him. He ran laterally, looking for a block somewhere. But the golden herd broke through. There was only one thing to do. Scotty cut back upfield, driving for every yard he could get. Then the avalanche buried him.

The ball was on the 11-yard line.

The Tigers huddled, surprised, some of them puzzled. Somebody growled, "What's the matter, Clayburn? What happened?"

Cowan said, "He fumbled the ball and kicked it into the end zone. Try to name a dumber play than that!"

Hodges snapped, "Let's cut the beefing!" He called Cowan on a handoff.

Cowan pounded into a moil of struggling linemen. He got a bare three yards. Hodges called Scotty's number. Scotty waited for the snap signal, burning with a desire to make up for that horrible misplay on the kickoff. He took the handoff and drove fiercely. A huge tackle lunged across his path, spinning him sideways.

The backer slammed him hard. It was third down and five.

There was urgency in Hodges' voice. "Let's get out of here! Block!" He called Scotty on a pitchout.

The Brighton end bruised past Burgamy's block. Scotty gave ground and got past the man, but the secondary swept in, piling him up. It was fourth and two.

They punted. Brighton brought it to their 47 and opened up a single-wing attack. They had a fleet-footed tailback and a hard-running fullback, and they poured blocking ahead of them. Scotty, assigned to safety on defense, found himself busy tackling runners who broke through.

Brighton moved to the Westland 20, first down. They sent the tailback wide. McGraw turned him in, and Cowan hit him. The ball plopped out of his hands, and Brooks fell on it.

So it was Westland's ball, and they had a chance to make capital of Brighton's error. But they got nowhere. They couldn't come untracked. Charging Brighton linemen turned their blocking efforts into a shambles. In three plays they got four yards. Scotty punted out of bounds on Brighton's 45.

And this time Brighton wouldn't be denied. They drove to Westland's 24 in nine bruising plays, then pulled one out of mothballs—the old "flea flicker." And it worked. When Hodges tackled the end who'd received the pass, the end flipped a lateral. The swift tailback took it and crossed the goal line unhampered.

Brighton chose to kick for one point. They made it.

139

The score was 7–0, and the stands were hushed in shocked disbelief.

The Tigers looked stunned too. Scotty knew they hadn't forgotten his boner—the fumble that had got them off to such a bad start. No doubt the crowd, too, was blaming him. Their imported talent, they were probably thinking, had turned out to be a very ordinary and overrated ball player.

The kickoff soared. Scotty waited to see that Cowan had it, then spurted in front of the ball carrier. A golden jersey loomed. Scotty threw a well-timed block into the man. He heard Cowan's cleats drumming by.

The block cleared a path for Cowan up the sideline. Farther upfield another block enabled him to cut back and keep going. Finally, somebody snagged an ankle and Cowan went down. But he'd gone all the way to the 40-yard line.

"Awright!" Cowan barked in the huddle. "This time we got a decent runback. Now let's go!"

McGraw drawled, "I guess you know who put the key in the door for you—or didn't you see Clayburn murder that guy?"

They began to move for the first time. Scotty got five on a quick opener. Burgamy lugged it four on a counter. Hodges sneaked for first down. Seven on a pitchout to Scotty. Five more on one to Cowan. On the outside handoff, the big tackle nailed Scotty, but on the next play Hodges' pass to McGraw was good. The redhead was tumbled on the 24.

Hodges said, "That left tackle has been crashing. Let's trap him."

It worked beautifully. Brighton had dropped into a tight 6–2–2–1. As Scotty took the ball, Dupre slaughtered the charging tackle. McLarty and Dent two-teamed the guard and wiped him out. Scotty burst through the gaping hole into the open.

One good downfield block now, and he'd have a touchdown. But no block materialized. Scotty cross-stepped, eluding the halfback, raced the safety man for the corner. The safety man was very fast. He closed the gap, hammering Scotty out of bounds. The ball was on the 2-yard line.

Hodges sent Cowan diving into the line. The referee dug into the pileup. The ball was over by inches. Touchdown!

Jeffers sent word to kick for the one point. They lined up. The crowd noise abated. The ball came back and Hodges set it down expertly. Head down, eye on the ball, Scotty kicked. The leather tumbled straight through the uprights. The game was tied at 7–7.

Brighton took the kickoff and turned on the power again. They eked out first downs. Then down on the Westland 19, Scotty stole a pass, and the drive was stopped.

They tried Burgamy on a slant, and he was smothered. Hodges said, "See that defense? We'll pass off the buck series."

It was a daring move, but Brighton, playing virtually an eight-man line with halfbacks in close, was set up for it. Hodges faked to Cowan, kept the ball. Scotty wheeled out, turned upfield with a sudden burst, and was behind the halfback. He turned his head, and the ball was there. He took it without breaking stride, and not a man got within five yards of him as he sprinted seventy more yards to the end zone.

The roars thundered down. The cheerleaders turned handsprings. It was the first spectacular play of the night, and the crowd was deliriously happy.

Scotty kicked the point, and they were ahead 14–7.

Doggedly, Brighton struck back. It became a battle of savage defenses that wouldn't give in the clutch. But it was Brighton who made the serious threats. Another pass interception by Clayburn thwarted one scoring bid; a costly fumble stopped a second one. But Brighton roared back again to reach the Westland 18 before the Tiger line dug in. Hodges was knocking down a last-second aerial attempt as the half ended.

It was still anybody's game.

Inside, the coaches moved among them quietly, checking minor hurts, pointing out flaws in individual play.

Then Jeffers called them together. "Brighton's mistakes beat them that half. They may not make any more. That seven points won't win this game, not if you keep letting them control the ball three-fourths of the time. Let's get out there and take it away from them—and get some tallies!"

Brighton was having something to say about that, however. They took the kickoff and moved to Westland's 23 before they had to give it up. They held Westland, forcing them to punt.

Then, at last, the Tiger defense stopped them cold

on their own 30. And Brighton made one more mistake: the punter kicked a low, fast one straight at Scotty Clayburn.

Scotty paced himself, giving his blockers time. Then as the pattern took shape, he shifted into high gear. A burst of speed carried him past one diving tackle. A lane opened up to the right. He shot through like a shaft of light, swerved in behind two screening white jerseys, and he was at midfield. He hit for the sideline. Two men thundered in to meet him.

He cut back sharply, away from one man, offered the other a tempting target with a change of pace. The tackler drove at him. Scotty, with an incredible gliding cross-step, reversed his field—and he was past everyone, still pulling away when he crossed the double stripe.

The stands were going crazy. Scotty flipped the ball to an official and turned to meet his grinning mates. To their praise, he replied, "I got the blocks at the right time. That made it easy."

"Easy, he says!" McGraw howled merrily.

After that there was plenty of action, but it was all anticlimax. It was the old story of a desperate team trying to play "catch-up," taking long chances, having them backfire in their faces. Brighton gambled on a flat pass deep in their own territory. Hodges snared it and ran straight down the sideline for a score. Minutes later Scotty picked off another Brighton pass and sifted through a broken field to the 14. On the fourth play, Burgamy carried it over from the 1-yard line.

With the score 34–7, Jeffers sent in a steady stream

of replacements. But Brighton's poise was shattered now, and the subs held them on even terms until the finish.

A happy, noisy crowd started pouring out of the stands. Fragments of conversation reached the players' ears as they filed up the ramp. "Another great team" . . . "Look better than last year's" . . . "Took a tough ball club tonight and made it look easy" . . . "You see that Clayburn! That's what I call stepping through the dew" . . . "Give you even money they win state" . . .

Scotty frowned in thought. They had a good team, yes. But that kind of talk! The truth was they'd been pretty lucky tonight. Take away Brighton's costly mistakes, and it would have been a close ball game. The crowd couldn't see that. But he knew it, and the rest of the team knew it.

Later, in the dressing room, he wasn't so sure. Somebody yelled, "Bring on Concho! We'll take those sheepherders just like we took this outfit!" A chorus of yells rang out in response. They were in a gay mood, as they had a right to be. Scotty felt good, too. It was always a great feeling to win. But there seemed to be something else in the atmosphere—the kind of confidence that bordered on cockiness. Maybe he was mistaken. He hoped so.

On the ride home, his uncle reflected the mood of the crowd. "You should have heard 'em in the stands, Scotty. They're already calling you our meal ticket to the state championship." He chuckled. "Yes, sir, you and that team are going all the way this year. Tell me, just how much better would you say this club is than last year's team—about two touchdowns?"

Scotty's first impulse was to evade the question. Then he decided he might as well take the opportunity to cool off some of his uncle's overoptimism. "We don't have the all-around balance of last year's team, Uncle John. Not yet anyway."

"Here now!" John Durham protested. "What kind of talk is that? What's wrong with this team?"

Scotty could have explained it. That sometimes a team could lose half its starters and still turn up with a better team, but that it hadn't happened this time. Four of their losses had been in the line—down there where your football is won or lost. And so far, nobody had truly replaced them. There were no Keegans or Beddos at tackle. Nobody who could back a line like Gaddis, or play end defense like Jacoby.

But he didn't want to call names to his uncle. Instead, he said, "Don't get me wrong. We've got a good team and we'll get better. I'm proud to be playing with them. It's just that—well, we're no super team. And it's bad for people to expect too much. Makes it tough for the players and the coach."

John Durham laughed. "Kid, you're a perfectionist. Just another reason this team is going to be the greatest!"

Scotty let it drop. But he knew there was a lot of hard work ahead before they were a championship team. And next week—only seven days away—they were meeting mighty Concho!

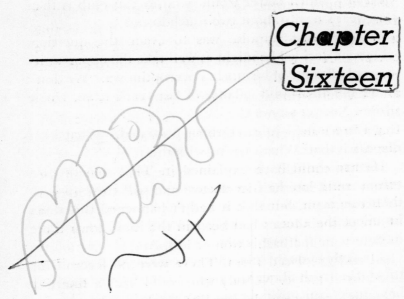

Scotty hadn't been too surprised to find his uncle and other fans overrating the team. But he was really puzzled when the newspapers did the same thing.

Even Carlton of the *Times* said, "Whoever beats the Tigers this year will win the state title." And Pinley went much further. At one point he wrote: "The Tigers played under wraps, waited for their foes' mistakes, then pounced with the sudden lethal punch of a jungle beast. It's the kind of team that's just as likely to score from 80 yards as 8—and the lad mainly responsible for that is a swivel-hipped phantom named Scotty Clayburn."

Both papers were lavish in their praise, making much of his 80-yard pass-and-run touchdown and his

72-yard punt return, passing lightly over the opening fumble. It was all very nice. You couldn't help feeling a pleasant sensation at being thus lauded in print. Yet Scotty knew it was the very thing that could hurt him most now. He was still new and, to some of them, still an outsider wearing a Tiger uniform. Some of the shadow he'd acquired last year still clung to him. Getting a lion's share of the spotlight wasn't going to help dispel it.

He had thought the sportswriters would detect the team's weak points and warn the public to reserve their judgment awhile. But now the whole town would be expecting them to knock over all opponents like dummies. And if they didn't . . .

Strangely enough, it was Esco Hammer who was able to see the truth about the team. "I see the promotion boys have you guys on the spot already," Esco said. "Boy, will they turn sour if you lose to Concho! And you're liable to, Scotty."

It was Saturday night, and Scotty had gone over to see how Esco was coming on his transceiver.

Scotty said, "We'll try to give them a battle."

Esco smiled. "Don't want to gossip about your team, do you? But you can't fool me. Some weak spots showed up out there last night."

"Then you saw the game last night?"

"I'll be seeing all of them this year. I might as well admit it—I'm a hopeless football fanatic again. And you're to blame. I have a feeling with you in the ball game that something exciting can bust loose any minute." Esco's expression changed suddenly. He gave

147

Scotty a solemn look. "Some people say I'm too nosy. But you'll admit I never did try to pump you last year about that trouble you had—that run-in with Cowan. Tell me, has the team got over that? Are you getting a fair shake from them this year?"

Scotty said warily, "Sure, we get along okay. That's all in the past, Esco."

"Is it?" Esco queried. "Okay, I'm prying now, I know. But there's something puzzles me. They said you were mad at the guy, threatened him. But nobody ever seemed to mention *why*. Now I'm sure of two things—you had no intention of injuring him, and if you were mad, you had a good reason. What reason? Why didn't that ever come out?"

"I suppose because I never did tell anybody."

Esco said quietly, "Would you tell me, Scotty? Or do you figure it's none of my business?"

For a long moment Scotty said nothing. It had been hard, keeping the thing shut up inside all this time. And here was someone he could confide in—and trust.

Finally, he said, "You will keep it to yourself?"

"Promise," Esco said.

Scotty told him. And somehow he felt relieved. It was like opening the floodgates of a dam.

When he finished, Esco said, "What a dirty thing for him to do! And nobody saw it?"

"That's right. Nobody."

"It's a crying shame he got away with it. But why in all creation didn't you tell them about it—tell the coach?"

"I had reasons," Scotty said. "It's hard to explain."

"Okay. I think I know." Esco squinted at him. "Scotty, you're a swell guy, but you're pretty bull-headed."

"Thanks for the compliment."

"And a little oversensitive too."

"Thanks again."

"All right, I'll shut up before you bop me. Now, if you're not too sore at me to stay, I'll show you my set."

"I'm not sore, Esco." Scotty smiled soberly. "Just hate to admit you might be right."

Esco grinned. "Okay, let's take a look. I got me a Heathkit, ten-meter band . . ."

At the Monday workout it was soon evident that the team was afflicted with overconfidence. Coach Jeffers recognized the symptoms at once—a bobbled handoff, a missed assignment, a general lack of attention. He stopped the workout and gave them some straight talk. They'd better forget what they'd read in the newspapers and get to work.

It helped a little. But the complacency was still there. There were a few exceptions. Scotty for one. And battle-wise Ceph Hodges and Red McGraw and Harry Dupre were on their toes, urging their mates to show more pepper. But their urgings went largely unheeded.

The coach was trying to do something about the tackle situation too. He shifted Dupre from guard to tackle, pulling out Ruthven and promoting Pete Sanchez at guard. Sanchez was small for a lineman but tough and quick-moving.

The next day Jeffers came up with a backfield

149

change. Dave Franklin was taken off the halfback list and tried out at fullback. They were long on halfback reserves, and Burgamy's blocking the week before at fullback had left much to be desired.

Dave was looking good at his new post, Scotty noted. The change seemed to give him fresh enthusiasm, new hope.

Scotty told him, "You know how I feel, Dave. I've nothing against Burgamy, but if you can beat him out, I'm sure for you."

"I'll take the job away from him if I can," Dave averred.

He might just do it, Scotty thought, if he felt that way about it. Dave was a pretty solid ball player, needing confidence as much as anything.

Jeffers worked them long and late that day. And still they were not jarred out of their smugness. On the way in from the field, McLarty, the right tackle, grumbled, "What a day! Coach must be trying to kill us off before Concho gets here!"

Scotty was walking on the fringe of the group. Like a reflex, the words came: "He's trying to save us from taking a country licking."

Cowan snorted. "Why worry? Any time we need a touchdown, we'll just hand you the ball. I read it in the papers."

Scotty tried to turn it off with a laugh. "Remember what Coach said about the stuff you read in the papers."

But that didn't end it. McLarty turned on Scotty.

150

"What makes you think Concho is going to beat us?"

Scotty wished he'd kept silent. Somebody needed to tell them, but he wasn't the one to do it. The issue was pushed on him now, though, and there was no retreating. He said, "I didn't say they'd beat us. But they will if we don't start hustling and get ready to go at top speed every minute."

"We'll be ready," McLarty said. "Concho doesn't scare me. So they beat Silver City sixty-eight to nothing. Who is Silver City? We beat a real ball club."

Scotty wanted to drop it. But the arrogance in McLarty's tone was too much. "Look, let's face it. Brighton was rugged, but they pulled enough boners to lose three ball games."

Herb Brooks, the center, said, "To hear you tell it, Clayburn, we're just a bunch of lucky bums."

"All except Clayburn," Cowan said mockingly. "He's good."

His mouth drawn in a taut line, Scotty said nothing.

McLarty looked at him. "You're a good ball player, Clayburn. But I don't think you've caught the Westland spirit. We haven't stacked up one of the best records in the state by low-rating ourselves."

Somebody else said, "The way I look at it, a guy ought to believe in his own team."

Scotty remained silent. He'd talked too much already. He'd had his say and had accomplished nothing —except to reopen an old rift between him and his teammates.

Why, he wondered, had they never really accepted

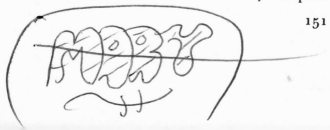

him as one of them? Several things, perhaps. His too-big share of publicity in the papers. The incident of Cowan's injury last year.

But the basic cause, he knew, was rooted in some-thing deeper. It went far back to that first story Pinley had published a year ago—and beyond that to the years when Westland's good name had been tarnished by a shameless flouting of the rules of fairness and good sportsmanship, by the "hiring" of football players. Westland students had become aware of that past, had come to hate it and resent it. And, thanks to Pinley, they associated Scotty Clayburn with it.

Illogical though it might be, he was identified in some vague way with the riffraff of that past era. And there wasn't much he could do about it—except to wait for the time when they would judge him fairly.

There was just one thing, he thought bitterly. How much longer did he have to wait?

Esco came over that night, ostensibly to study with him on a unit test. But it was soon apparent that he had something else on his mind.

As they settled down in Scotty's room, Esco said abruptly, "I've been thinking about that thing last year, when Cowan chopped you on the neck. You've been assuming something all along, Scotty, that may not be true."

"Meaning what?"

"That nobody else on the team knows it. Hasn't it ever occurred to you that some other player *might* have seen it happen?"

The idea was a startling one to Scotty. He'd never once considered it. "No," he finally said. "I'm sure no one saw it."

"How do you know that?"

"They'd have said something when Cowan accused me."

"Why are you so sure?" Esco persisted.

"I just know. None of the fellows would—" He stopped, suddenly realizing he wasn't sure, not absolutely sure.

"See what I mean? Now, tell me something. Who was in a position on the field where it was possible for him to see it?"

"A lot of the boys. I mean it's hard to tell—"

"It happened twice. What man close to the play had the best chance to see it at least one of those times? Think back. Try to re-create a picture of the action in your mind."

"I can't remember. Look, Esco, I don't want to start suspecting somebody just because—"

"Can you draw me a diagram of the play?"

"Yes. But a play on paper and what happens on the field—it's not always the same."

"Draw it anyway, Scotty—just to humor me, huh?"

"Okay." Scotty sighed. "Just to humor you."

"And write the names on the defense team," Esco added.

Scotty drew the diagram, trying to indicate as accurately as he could where each man would be as he reacted to the movement of the play.

Esco studied the circles and X marks carefully. He

pointed to an X. "I'd say this player, more than anybody else, was in a position to see it."

Scotty looked. "You're all wrong. He was captain, a leader—not the kind of guy to cover up—" His voice trailed off. Things began to jump into his mind. That afternoon, when they'd come in and learned about Cowan's broken rib, Fred Gaddis, captain, supposed leader, had been strangely quiet. Now that he thought about it, he couldn't remember Gaddis saying a word. You'd think he would have entered into the discussion some way. And Gaddis had quarreled with Julie—maybe because she was giving Scotty too much attention?

No. His imagination was running wild. It was crazy. Esco's whole idea was crazy.

"Of course," Esco was saying, "there are others, two in particular, who are possibles. But by the laws of probability—"

"I still say *nobody* saw it. Anyway, suppose they did. How could we ever prove it? And what good would it do?" Scotty smiled ruefully. "What I needed was a movie camera on that other play—the one when I hit Cowan."

Esco looked at him. "You mean it wouldn't help any if we could prove what Cowan did to you?"

Scotty frowned. "I don't know, Esco. I'd rather just forget it." Those ideas about Fred Gaddis—they'd never entered his mind before. He wished it could have stayed that way.

"Yeh, I guess it wasn't such a good idea," Esco said.

"Anyway, Gaddis is off to college. So are Leighton and Beddo."

He seemed to dismiss it from his mind as quickly as he'd brought it up. Scotty hoped he could do the same.

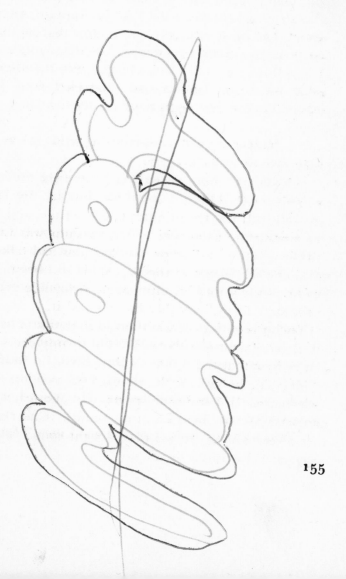

Chapter
Seventeen

It was ten minutes to game time, and not a seat among the 21,000 in Tiger Stadium was vacant.

This was the game! For days the fans had talked of nothing else. "Game of the Week," it had been called by one of the state's big-city papers. "Possible preview of the state finals," another had termed it.

Concho's contingent was there, two thousand strong, noisily confident of victory. Westland supporters were just as sure that the ninety miles to Concho would be a "long ride home" for the vanquished tonight.

A roar swelled from the spectators. The teams were emerging from beneath the stands. Cheerleaders turned cartwheels. Bands played fight songs. The air was charged with tension.

Concho won the toss and chose to receive. Scotty took his position. His job was to hold back as safety man on the kickoff. Dupre would do the booting.

The scarlet-and-black Concho Raiders deployed to receive. They were not an overly big team—except for Ben Dulin, monstrous 230-pound tackle and defensive middle guard. But they were big enough, and they were fast and agile—and rawhide tough.

Scotty studied them, seeking out four men in particular. He had identified the four in the pregame warm-up. Benny Wingo, lean-limbed, fleet halfback; Rufe Rawdon, dark and muscular fullback; Tom Peninger, rangy end with the meat-hook hands; Len Burkett, big and blocky tackle.

These were Concho's famous recruits. Each one had been hand-picked, his family moved to Concho, the father given a job. After a year of seasoning—and waiting for eligibility—they were now spotted in key positions on the first team. This was Concho's answer to the transfer rule. There was no secret about it. Everybody in the state who followed football knew that a certain group of men in the oil town had made sure that their team would be "loaded" again this year.

Dupre advanced on the ball. The kick went to Murphy, Raider quarterback, in the corner. Murphy took off on a wide slant to the left. Westland jerseys converged in that direction.

Scotty yelled a warning. They'd been coached to watch for this!

It had been neatly done. Benny Wingo, coming like a wraith out of a fog, had crossed paths with Murphy.

There had been a deft exchange of the ball, and now Wingo had it and was running like a frightened deer in the opposite direction. McGraw and Hodges had recovered, but a little late, and suddenly Wingo had only Scotty Clayburn between him and the goal line.

It was a race for the sideline. Scotty closed the gap. Wingo feinted a cutback, pulled wide again. The trick didn't work. Scotty's tackle sent the pair of them hurtling off the field of play. The ball was on Westland's 47-yard line.

The Raiders lined up in a tight T. The Scarlet backfield shuttled into baffling motion that hid the ball from sight. Then Rawdon emerged with the leather on a sweep. He got outside Hollum's end and cut upfield. High-stepping knees tore him away from Brooks's tackle. Burgamy went down under a block. Rawdon veered, running straight at Scotty a moment, trying to freeze him. But as Rawdon swerved out again, Scotty hit him, pinning the pistoning legs together.

Scotty got up, fingering a bruise on his cheek where an errant elbow had cracked him. Rawdon looked at him, a touch of curiosity in flat, almost expressionless eyes, then turned away.

It was first down on Westland's 32. The Raiders poured raw power at them. In five plays it was first and goal on the 8. Hodges called time out.

They talked it over, trying to encourage one another. But their words carried no conviction. They hadn't been ready for this game. Now the poison of overconfidence was having its reaction, leaving them shaken and uncertain.

They went into a tight goal-line defense. But they did not stop Concho. Emery, Raider right half, dived inside tackle for four. Then, on a cleverly faked cross-buck, Emery pitched out to Wingo. Rawdon's explosive block obliterated Hodges, and Wingo skirted wide for the touchdown.

The Raiders went for two points. Rawdon plowed on a power plunge and made it. The score was 8–0.

Still dazed, the Tigers spread out to receive. Burgamy reached for a low, skidding kickoff, and the ball slipped off his hands. He picked it up again, and a tackler hit him. The ball shot free. Cowan dived for it, but a Raider was there first, cuddling the leather under his scarlet jersey.

It was Concho's ball on the Westland 16-yard line.

They scored in two plays. First, a thunderous blast by Rawdon to the 9. Then a rollout by Murphy, who followed a crushing wave of blockers across the goal line. They kicked this time, and it was good. Westland was down 15–0, and they hadn't had the ball yet!

The Concho cheering section was going wild. The rest of the stands was wrapped in gloomy silence.

Cowan got the kickoff and was stopped on the 22. They met in the huddle, grim-faced. Hodges' voice was hoarse. "Let's play some football now. Move 'em out on twenty-two!"

Scotty took the handoff and drove. It was like running into a steel trap. Burkett hadn't been moved an inch; neither had Dulin. They buried Scotty at the line of scrimmage.

Cowan hit tackle for two. On a running pass option,

159

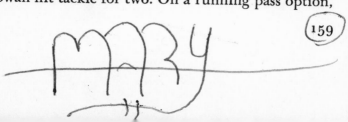

Scotty threw just as Rawdon hit him. He got up, groggy for a moment. That Rawdon sure was handy with his elbows. But the pass had been complete to McGraw. They had first down on the 36.

They got no farther. The Raiders stopped Cowan. They stopped Burgamy. They broke up Hodges' pass to Hollum.

Scotty punted, and the Raiders marched again. Behind the line, Cowan and Brooks battled to plug the holes, but the Raider backs speared the frontal defense, and it was left to the tertiary to bring them down. Scotty was everywhere, fighting on all fronts. Twice he prevented imminent touchdowns as the speedy Wingo burst into the open. He gambled on hunches, aided tackles close to the line. But the Raiders kept coming.

They reached the 16, then sprung Rawdon wide. Hollum and Brooks and Burgamy were wiped out. Rawdon cut in behind two blockers who'd streamed across. It was a sure touchdown.

Except the blockers waited a split instant too long. Scotty moved with the speed of forked lightning. He streaked between the two men, hurled himself at Rawdon's churning knees. The fullback's legs flew up and he nose-dived to the turf.

Rawdon stared at Scotty with grudging respect. "You're pretty tough, little man," he said without emotion. "But you're going to do that one time too many."

They stopped the Raiders then, but only with the aid of a 15-yard holding penalty. Westland took over on the 3-yard line. They couldn't move the ball and had to punt.

And a minute later Concho had another score. Wingo took a pass in the flat and went all the way to the 2 before Scotty hauled him down from behind. On the first plunge Rawdon carried it over. The kick was a fraction wide, and it was 21–0.

Complaint rumbled through the Westland stands. What was wrong out there? Why hadn't Jeffers got them ready for this game? Maybe Jeffers was losing his touch. That Concho outfit was really a machine. That Al Zerner of Concho was a coach!

The kickoff rode the breeze clear out of the end zone, and they lined up on the 20. Scotty faked a run and passed to McGraw for nine. Then, on the same play, Scotty saw the secondary holding back, and he tucked in the ball and took off. Dave was in now at fullback, and the block he laid on Peninger gave Scotty a special sort of thrill. He faked Rawdon off his feet and kept going. Somebody bumped him off balance, and Emery cut him down. But they were up to the 41.

Cowan roared for twelve on a reverse, and they were in Concho territory at last. They worked it down to the 23, clicking for the first time. Then, slamming inside tackle, Cowan was hit by three men—and the ball flew free. Dulin fell on it. Concho's ball!

Rawdon came off tackle. He slashed through the secondary and emerged like an enraged buffalo, running straight at Scotty. As they crashed down together, a knee jerked up, raking Scotty's jaw, and everything went dim for a while.

Jim Boone was bending over him. He felt a sudden

fear that he would be removed from the game. "No, Coach! I'm okay."

"Maybe," Jim Boone said. "Let's see you walk around."

They left him in. Concho promptly sent a pass into his zone, figuring he might still be dazed. Scotty jumped with Peninger and knocked it down. But the Raiders rolled on. Then, down on the 30, Rawdon blasted off tackle, and this time Cowan hit him. And Cowan did not get up. Moments later they helped him off the field, his head hanging groggily.

Burgamy took over the backer-up spot. Wingo buzzed wide to the 15. Rawdon blasted to the 10. Hodges called time out.

They gathered, a badly mauled crew, weary, disheartened. Hodges said, "We gotta stop 'em. They score again and we're sunk."

Nobody replied for a moment. It was plain they considered themselves beaten already. Defeat was written on their faces.

McLarty said, "We gotta stop that Rawdon. He's murdering us. He runs or throws a key block on every play."

"That," Brooks said, "is like stopping a dump truck."

Dupre said, "Anybody want to try Burkett? I'll trade him to you for Rawdon."

Scotty could keep his silence no longer. "So we're giving up. We might as well call off the game and go home."

McLarty bristled. "What's the meaning of that crack?"

"It means we're out here to play a football game—and the game's not over yet." Scotty hadn't meant to say this much, but the feeling in him was too strong to hold back now. "There're a few thousand kids counting on us to look like a Westland team is supposed to look. I always thought that meant playing the game all out till the last gun."

They stared at him. The marks of a physical battering were on him. His jersey was sweat-soaked and grimy. One cheek was puffed out with a great ugly bruise, and the other was trickling blood from a fresh cut. But his jaw was steady, and his eyes were bright with a sort of clear, clean anger.

Red McGraw smiled with grim humor. "You know, pals, this is something. This kid comes to school here and keeps his nose clean and tends to his knitting. For that he gets the snubs and the ice treatment and a few nasty words here and there. And after all that, he's the only one of us that's mad and ashamed because Westland is losing a ball game."

They stood there, stunned for a moment. Then Herb Brooks growled, "Who says he's the only one! I've got just as much Westland spirit as Clayburn. I want to win this game too."

"That goes for me," McLarty said. "And for all the rest of us if I know this team."

Harry Dupre said, "The best way we could prove that would be to do what Clayburn says—stop the crybaby talk and start playing football."

Tom Dent said quietly, "That makes sense to me."

Hodges added, "Let's do it then. Seven-four, tackles and ends tight. And remember, we want that football!"

The Raiders must have wondered what hit them. Wingo took a pitchout and was swarmed for a yard loss. Rawdon stabbed at the middle and got a scant yard. Emery was stopped cold. Murphy went back to pass and was smothered in his tracks. Westland took over on the 16-yard line.

Scotty took a handoff, and the hole was there this time, large and beautiful. He went for ten big yards. Earl Hanna, now in for Cowan, bolted through for six more. Hodges ran the keeper for five. They kept going, reaching the Concho 36 with a first down. But time was running out now. They must strike for a quick score.

On a running pass, Scotty flipped to McGraw for eleven. They were still twenty-five yards away, with forty seconds left. Hodges turned to the air, and Concho sent four rushers in on him. Hard-pressed, he sailed two tosses a yard beyond the receiver's hands. A third throw was knocked down. On the fourth Scotty, coming out of a flanker, cut across behind McGraw's buttonhook fake and pulled down the flying leather.

He took one stride, and Wingo hit him. He kept driving, carrying the tackler with him. Then Murphy hit him from the other side, and Scotty went down. He lay there a moment, sick with disappointment. The ball was less than a yard short of the goal line.

Before he could get up, the gun went off.

It was quiet in the dressing room. Scotty lay on a mat, letting the brief rest restore his spent strength. He was trying to forget that last play, forget everything for just a little while.

Before the buzzer sounded, Jeffers called them together. "I don't know what happened those last few minutes. Whatever it was, you looked like a different team—" He stopped, his eye drawn to a rustle of movement among the players.

"Excuse us, Coach." Harry Dupre, his hand on Rex Cowan's arm, stepped out. "I think Rex has something to tell us."

Jeffers gave them a narrow look. "Okay. What is it?"

Cowan faced them, a sort of trapped yet doggedly determined look in his eyes. "I figure I should clear up something that's given a lot of people some wrong ideas. It's about—last year when I got my rib broken. It was an accident—and mostly my own fault. I should know better, but I went in there with my arms high, and when Clayburn blocked me, well, he hit me so quick I didn't get my arms down, and his shoulder slammed into my ribs. It was just a clean block—hard, but clean."

A heavy silence filled the room.

"There's something else." Cowan darted a look toward Dupre, went on. "Before that happened, I'd been hacking Clayburn on the neck, chopping him with the side of my hand—" He paused, lowering his eyes.

Scotty wasn't looking at Cowan. He was looking at Dupre. And in that instant, something in Dupre's eyes

—a sort of grimness—told Scotty everything in one revealing flash.

So Esco had been right after all! Somebody *had* seen it. Not Gaddis—Scotty felt a rush of shame for suspecting the former captain—but Dupre! And Dupre had reached a point where he could keep it to himself no longer. So he'd given Cowan a choice: Cowan could come clean or he, Dupre, would spill it himself.

Cowan was saying, "—is why he was so sore at me. I don't know why he never told anybody. Maybe he thought I'd do the right thing and own up to it. . . . Well, I'm telling you now and I'm apologizing to him— and the team."

A murmur rose in the room but stopped suddenly when Dupre said, "Now I'll take my turn. I've known this all the time. I was pulling out, following the play, and I saw Clayburn catch that blow on the neck. Sure, I've been a heel, keeping quiet all this time. I—well, I've played with Rex since we were in junior high and . . . but that's no excuse. I have no excuse. We both did a wrong thing to a mighty right guy."

Jeffers, his eyes stern, said slowly, "Yes, Harry, you did do a wrong thing." He turned to Cowan. "I hope you realize, Rex, that your confession has come a little too late to undo all the harm you did an innocent boy."

Cowan nodded dumbly, saying nothing.

"I'm starting you back in there this half," Jeffers said. "But I want you to understand—this business of last year is not a closed matter."

The coach was assuming, Scotty was sure, that

Cowan had come forward to unburden his conscience. And Jeffers was weighing what he thought was a voluntary confession against the conviction that Cowan should not go entirely unpunished.

Scotty hoped the coach would accept the apology at full value and let the whole matter drop as quietly as possible. A harsh penalty against Cowan would bring on a new rash of gossip and publicity, could even stir some backlash of resentment against Scotty, as well as the coach. It was a thing Scotty did not want to see happen. But the decision, of course, would have to rest with Jeffers.

Ceph Hodges raised a hand. "Can I say a word, Coach?"

"Go ahead," Jeffers said quietly.

"You wondered what happened out there a while ago. I'll tell you. We were about ready to give up, and Scotty Clayburn stirred us up and made us ashamed of ourselves. We hated to admit it, but—well, I guess he showed us he had more of the old Westland spirit than any man of us."

"And we better hope he can forgive us," Herb Brooks said. "Because we're lucky to have him on our side."

"You can say that again!" McLarty said. "But it sure took some of us hardheads a long time to find it out."

Scotty was too full of emotion to speak. He'd waited so long for this, it was hard to realize it was really happening. He was no longer an outsider. He belonged. And the best of it was, all the bitter hurt was gone, buried with the past. He felt only pride in being one of them at last.

Jeffers said, "Thanks, Ceph, for the explanation." His voice rose. "And now, men, I believe we have an appointment on the field with the Concho ball club."

The tension snapped. Red McGraw boomed, "Let's go get 'em, gang!" There was a loud chorus of agreement. . . .

Westland lined up for the kickoff, eager and ready. But they were facing the task with their eyes open now. They knew it would be tough. They had their work cut out for them—getting back 21 points in two quarters.

The kick went to Cowan, and the big boy ran with fierce determination, bowling off two tacklers before he was ganged on the 32.

They went to work. Dave, still in at fullback, plunged for eight big yards. On a trap Scotty clipped off ten. Then he shot a running pass to Cowan, moving them to the Concho 41. Hodges kept and gained seven, then passed to McGraw for eight. Concho called time out to talk it over.

Westland went to the flanker formation. Scotty buttonhooked and took a pass from Hodges. He spun away from Emery, cutting back toward the opposite side of the field. Rawdon was pursuing him, Wingo closing the gap in front. Scotty veered with a fluid motion, never slackening speed, leaving both of them behind. Murphy came in warily. And when the tackler moved, Scotty cross-stepped and shot out a straight-arm. He sprang free, regained stride, and crossed the goal line. The stands went crazy.

They lined up as if to kick, but the ball went to Scotty. He passed to McGraw for two points. It was 21–8.

An aroused Concho struck with a crunching ground attack. Slowly, like a scarlet tide, they advanced. Then down inside the 10, the Tigers clawed them to a halt.

Hodges played it safe, staying on the ground. Three plunges were a foot short of first down. And for once Scotty failed to point the kick away from Wingo. The speedster rode a wave of blocking to the 28 before Scotty nailed him.

Suddenly, the Raiders struck through the air. Peninger, racing deep, reached for the pass. Scotty leaped, slapping the ball. There was a sideswiping collision, and as he hit the ground he stared with a sick feeling. Wingo had picked the ball off the grasstops and was careening into the end zone.

It was a cruel break, but the six points counted just the same. The kick made it 28–8. The Tigers, with little more than a quarter left, were right back where they'd started.

They fought to get it back. Scotty swirled and dodged forty yards with the kickoff. They ran the ends, sliced at the line, sprinkled in a pair of spot passes to reach the 9-yard line. Then it got tough. On fourth down Scotty got outside the end and raced for the corner. He bounced off Rawdon's tackle, but Emery slammed him out of bounds on the 3-yard line.

The Raiders played ball control, using up the precious minutes. Then, essaying surprise, they sent Peninger flaring out for a pass. Peninger's hands went up.

A slender figure flashed across his path, taking the ball on a dead run. The crowd came to its feet as Scotty Clayburn streaked for the sideline. Rawdon, meeting him at the crossroads, launched a savage tackle. Scotty reversed his field, and Rawdon crashed empty-handed. Murphy loomed, and Scotty pulled wide again. Murphy dived, fell short. Then out of nowhere came Wingo. He leaped, catching an ankle. Scotty stumbled heavily, and for a moment he knew he must fall. But somehow he got his feet under him again, and he was all alone, sprinting ahead of the pack for a touchdown. The roar was like thunder.

On the conversion, Hodges faked a pass, and Cowan took the ball off his hands and swept inside the flag untouched.

So it was 28–16, but there were less than six minutes, and Concho hoarded the ball. Westland stopped the steamroller drive at midfield and took over on the 20 after a punt over the goal line. Hodges started passing. Three throws went awry, two were knocked down, but four were complete—to Scotty and to McGraw—and they were down to the Concho 22. Again Hodges threw the ball. McGraw cut in, reaching for it.

Wingo came like a thief in the night. He stole the ball and was gone in a blur of lateral motion, gathering blockers like magic. White jerseys tumbled and Wingo flashed into the open, sweeping over the white lines like a whirlwind across a prairie—and into the end zone. Concho kicked, and it was 35–16.

And there was only one minute left.

The Tigers fought to the end. They filled the air with passes that carried them quickly downfield. But they did not score. They were on the Concho 18 when the gun went off.

They went in, tired and disappointed, but no longer ashamed. Among them, only Hodges was gloomy. "I was throwing lousy," he moaned. "Scotty was open twice if I'd hit him."

"Don't blame yourself," McGraw said. "You didn't lose the ball game. We all lost it. We were too cocky at the start."

"Just what Coach was trying to tell us," Dupre observed.

Brooks added, "Also Clayburn—if you remember."

"How right he was!" McLarty said. He turned to Scotty. "I hope you can forget all those stupid cracks I made."

"What cracks?" Scotty smiled innocently.

McGraw said, "We lost a ball game, but we learned a lesson. We'll go to work now. And we'll have a real ball club."

Which summed it up pretty neatly, Scotty thought.

Chapter
Eighteen

In his study-hall period Monday, Scotty received a call slip from the coach's office. When he arrived, Cowan was already there.

Jeffers said, "Rex and I have been having a talk, Scotty. He wants to say something to you."

Cowan's once-arrogant eyes were solemn and subdued. He said, "It was a dirty thing I did to you, Clayburn. I'm real sorry about it."

"Sure, I know," Scotty said. "You said so before."

"I wanted to say it to you—personally."

Scotty wondered if he imagined it, or was there just a touch of sincerity in Cowan's voice? He said, "I appreciate that."

There was an awkward silence. Cowan shuffled nervously, looking at Jeffers. "Shall I go back to class now, sir?"

Jeffers nodded. "You may go."

When Cowan was gone, Jeffers said, "I've made a decision, Scotty. As things stand now, Cowan is still on the team."

It meant, Scotty knew, that Cowan had been very close to suspension. What Jeffers had interpreted as a change of heart was all that had saved Cowan. Maybe there really had been a change of heart. A little, at least. Scotty wondered if he'd ever know for certain.

He said, "I'm glad about that, sir."

"I thought perhaps you would be." Jeffers gave Scotty a long, thoughtful look. "I wish you'd confided in me last year, Scotty."

"Yes, sir. I suppose I should have."

"Well, let's not worry about it now. I think things will work out." His tone lightened. "Okay for now, Scotty. See you at three-fifteen."

Scotty left with a sense of relief. He couldn't honestly feel any special love for Cowan. But no matter what the provocation, if Cowan had been dismissed from the squad, it would have left a bitter after-taste he could never have quite forgotten. . . .

The newspapers did not share the team's new optimism. The *Times* had pictured the game as a rout which could have been worse if Concho hadn't "eased up" in the second half. Pinley, with less restraint, had called it "the collapse of Westland's castle of championship dreams" and said "it was evident that the

Tigers didn't belong on the same field with the Scarlet Raiders."

Apparently, however, the players weren't paying much attention to the newspapers this time. High spirits, along with purpose and determination, were reflected in the way everyone hustled through the Monday workout.

One thing that afternoon disturbed Scotty a little, though. He noticed his uncle and two other men watching from the sideline. That in itself wasn't unusual. There were always spectators at workouts, including his uncle occasionally. But it was the intent—almost grim—way these men watched that bothered Scotty. And the fact that one of them was King Carruth.

Later, as they rode home, Scotty said, "I noticed Mr. Carruth out today. The other man a board member too?"

"Yes," his uncle said. "Gid Foutz, also newly elected to the board. Both of them are very interested in football. In fact, they're the board's new athletic committee."

Just what that meant Scotty wasn't sure. But he didn't like the looks of it. Carruth had never watched workouts before, not before the loss to Concho. And Carruth was a member of the win-or-else faction. A powerful member now that he could exert influence where it counted—on the school board.

It was Wednesday night when Scotty first got wind of the "rumor." He'd gone over to check some class notes with Esco. Also to check another thing. He hadn't had a chance to talk privately with his friend since the game.

Esco beat him to it. "So Dupre made Cowan talk."

"That's the way I figure it," Scotty said. "So you know what happened between halves?"

"Everybody knows. You know how those things leak out." Esco smiled. "Only they don't know Dupre prodded Cowan into talking. That's an angle only you and I figured out."

"I've been thinking the last day or so, Esco. Maybe Coach saw through it too."

"It would figure. Jeffers is a smart man."

"Coach hasn't said much. But I'm pretty sure Cowan is on probation."

"Behaving himself, huh?"

"Never saw him work harder and say less. Several fellows mentioned it to me. McGraw said maybe Cowan would be a better ball player, as well as a better guy, from now on."

"That's open to doubt," Esco said.

"You have to give the guy credit. He didn't enjoy doing it, but he came clean all the way, even about the injury. I didn't know myself just what happened when I hit him. I don't think we'll ever be buddy-buddies, but we'll work together." Scotty paused. "Esco, did you have anything to do with this?"

Esco grinned. "Matter of fact, I did have a plan. I was going to approach each of my suspects and say, 'What's the penalty for chopping a guy on the neck? Somebody told me you'd be the one to know all about it.' Then, if I got a guilty reaction, I'd keep making comments, maybe get them to wondering how much I knew, and just maybe they'd decide to spill it. But I never did do it, Scotty."

"I'm glad you didn't. Now we know it was conscience, not fear, that made Dupre decide."

Esco said, "Now I'll give you something new to worry about. You hear about the Touchdown Club reorganizing on the quiet?"

Scotty tensed. "No. And I hope it's just a rumor."

"It's a mighty persistent rumor. The way it goes, some of the town's sturdy citizens are getting organized to look around for football players—and bring pressure on the board to change its policy. Look at Concho, they're saying. Concho went out after some boys and see what they got."

"Where do you get all that stuff?"

"Partly from what Dad hears downtown. Also, I've got a very talkative barber."

Scotty shrugged. "Sounds like a lot of gossip to me."

But it worried him. So much so that the next night he questioned his uncle about it point-blank.

John Durham smiled. "People talk a lot—especially after the team loses a game."

"A thing like that would tear down everything Coach Jeffers has been building here. It . . . it's just not right."

His uncle's eyes narrowed. "You're taking it too seriously, Scotty. After all, if somebody wants to help a kid who'd like to attend a better school, why not? That's why *you* came here, you know."

Scotty turned a deep red.

"I wouldn't say you're doing this school any harm," his uncle went on. "Forget it, kid."

But Scotty couldn't get it off his mind. Uncle John had been evasive. It was evident that something was in the wind—and his uncle was not against it. Perhaps he was even a part of it!

And again the question came back to haunt him: If he hadn't been a football player, would his uncle have helped him come to Westland? It was a question that kept him awake that night long after he should have been asleep.

The lesson learned in the Concho game began to pay off that week. It was a hungry, alert team that took the field at Fort Worth against the Forest Park Lions. The Lions fought hard, but in the second quarter their defense crumbled before the fierce blocking of the vastly improved Westland line. Jeffers used every man on the bench, and the final score was 28–0.

The Westland team rode out to Fairdale the next Friday and coasted to a 49–0 victory. Again, the entire squad got a workout.

They came back and started getting ready for Kimball. This would be the big one—the district opener. From now on the games would count in the league standings.

This would be the test, the papers said. How far had the Tigers come since that crushing loss to Concho? Their last two opponents hadn't been strong enough to give the answer.

The game was played at Tiger Stadium. And it was a game that had the crowd on its feet from the opening whistle.

The first thrill came on the second play. It was a simple handoff, but one of those times when everything went right. Scotty bolted through the line and was in the open before a startled defense knew what had happened. He simply outsprinted the one man in his vicinity, cruising 64 yards for a touchdown.

Scotty felt a special exhilaration. His first game for Westland that counted in the standings—and he'd scored the first time he laid a hand on the ball!

He didn't have long to dwell on it. Using an intricate spread, Kimball opened up a passing barrage that took them to Westland's 22-yard line. Then they pulled a nifty—a play that had all the marks of a pass, then turned into a run and finally a reverse. The right half, who ended up with the ball, skimmed over the goal line without a hand being laid on him.

The fans were still standing moments later when Cowan burst through tackle for 34 yards to the Kimball 5 and Hodges sent Scotty wide on the next play for a touchdown. The mad pace slowed for a while as both teams stalled after long marches. Then the same Kimball right half, a very fast boy, picked off a Hodges pass in the flat and raced 90 yards to score.

That was the pattern for the night. It was a scoring bout. With six minutes left, the count was an incredible 28–28, and Westland was driving again. Almost stalled inside the 20, they shook Cowan loose on a trap. He picked up a key block by McGraw and went over standing up.

Kimball came right back, moving nearly sixty yards in nine plays. Then Hodges leaped in the end zone to steal a pass, and the Tigers held the ball till the gun. It was 35–28, and they had a victory in their first district game.

But it had been too close for comfort, and they were grateful to win.

"The best spread we'll see this year," McGraw said.

Dupre sang out, "One down, five to go!"

McLarty grinned. "But let's take 'em one at a time."

There was no false confidence now, Scotty knew. But they believed in each other. They were a team. From now on they'd be hard to stop.

Nothing had happened to alter the coach's decision on Cowan. The big halfback was showing a remarkable control of his hasty mouth and temper, and he was playing great ball.

In the weeks that followed, Westland knocked off one team after another. The going wasn't always easy. Scotty was now a marked man, with a special defense set to stop him. Yet he managed to come up with at least one long run in every game.

And when he was stopped, Cowan broke loose. Dave, a regular at fullback now, had developed into a fine blocker. The line was getting tougher and smarter every week.

So they marched down the victory road. They beat Hansford 29–7, San Palo 21–0, Calden 20–6, Dorado

35–12. Then in the last district game they overcame a stubborn Kingston team 13–0. And they were in the playoffs for the state title!

In those weeks a new life had opened up for Scotty Clayburn. Everywhere he went it was "Hi, Scotty. Great game, kid." . . . "Beautiful run the other night, Scotty." . . . "Come over to my house Saturday night, Scotty. Having a party." . . . When the team was introduced at pep assemblies, the calling of his name always brought thunderous and prolonged applause.

It was nice, but he knew it was mostly the adulation of the crowd for a football star. Much more important were the close friendships among those on the team and in his classes.

The newspapers were on the bandwagon now, voicing no doubts or criticism. Rumors about the Touchdown Club had died down. There were faint rumblings —that with that Clayburn kid in there, Jeffers should have a higher-scoring team. But the howl of the wolves had subsided to a mere whisper.

The team rode a plane four hundred miles out to Burk City for the bidistrict game. It was doped a shoo-in for the Tigers. The western-border town had a modest record against frail opposition.

But that day Burk City was a different team. With nothing to lose, they gambled on freak defenses. They played inspired football. And, unbelievably, at the half they led 15–14.

Jeffers was calm in the dressing room. He showed his men how to exploit the unorthodox defenses. They went back, and for a few minutes it looked as if they would run their opponents off the field. In six plays they were on Burk City's 8-yard line. Then, all at once, the drive lost its steam. There was an argument in the huddle, something that had never happened before. They drew a five-yard penalty for too much time. Hodges' pass was slapped down in the end zone, and the ball went over.

This was typical of their play on into the fourth period. They made a lot of yards; but always on the key play, something went wrong—a missed block, a faulty handoff. Not once again did Burk City threaten. Westland threatened constantly, but could not score.

Four minutes were left when Scotty intercepted a pass near midfield. And as he dashed upfield he thought: This could be it—the last chance.

He weaved a broken path through a field of enemy jerseys. Three times they laid hands on him, and each time his chopping, dancing legs tore him free. At last help arrived. It was Dave Franklin, slicing down a tackler. Scotty pulled wide and outsped the one remaining defender to cross the goal line.

They went for two points on a pass but failed. It was 20–15. And that was the ball game.

They were leaving the field, disgusted, relieved it was over. Dupre muttered, "Boy, am I glad we got that lousy game out of our system!"

McGraw said, "We can thank Scotty it wasn't worse!"

Scotty didn't hear either of them. His attention was fixed on a figure walking down the exit steps. A big man with beetle brows. Under those brows the eyes

181

were glowering with raw, dark anger. King Carruth was plainly unhappy.

The reason, Scotty figured, was simple. Mr. Carruth had doubtless lost a large wager on today's game, since Westland had been picked to win by 20 points. Probably his ego had also suffered quite a blow. And now Mr. Carruth had the look of a man who was out to make somebody pay for those injuries.

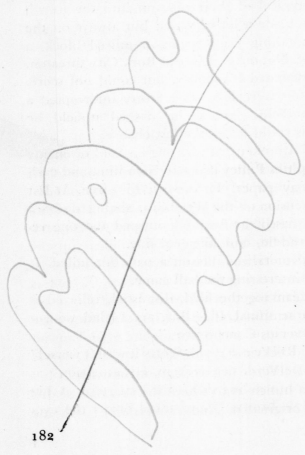

Chapter
Nineteen

Spinks Pinley dropped his little bombshell in the Tuesday paper. He wrote of "well-founded reports of dissension on the Westland team." He elaborated on the "fiasco" at Burk City, wrote of "quarreling" in the huddle, and in general summed up the Tigers as "a demoralized, floundering ball club."

"It will be interesting to see," he wrote, "if Jeffers can bring his team together this week before they meet Cliffton in the semifinal. If he doesn't, it's almost sure to be Cliffton versus Concho in the state final. Concho romped over Rockview 55–0 Saturday, and they'll probably take DelVerde this week almost as easily."

Scotty had a hunch as to where the "reports of dissension" had originated. And conversation with his uncle verified the suspicion. There'd been a board meeting the night before, his uncle told him. King Carruth had brought a report from the athletic committee—himself and Gid Foutz. Jeffers had "lost his hold on the boys," Carruth told other members of the board, and there was "bickering on the team."

So Carruth had gone to work. And his approach was clever. The board wouldn't fire a man merely for not winning a championship. But if he wasn't handling the boys properly, the board would be quite concerned.

Scotty said, "Surely the board won't fall for that."

His uncle smiled. "King is a mighty persuasive fellow."

Scotty's anger made him forget caution. "Don't they see his motive? Don't they know his past record—that he was a big wheel in the old Touchdown Club—and that those men—"

Now he'd said it. He reddened with embarrassment, but his eyes met those of his uncle, unflinching.

John Durham's smile faded. "I'm afraid Pinley gave you some melodramatic ideas about the Touchdown Club, Scotty. It was nothing more than a group of men supporting the football program. The fact is, we need an organization like that now. I don't know of another town our size that doesn't have some kind of a town football club."

Scotty felt a sort of bleak emptiness. There was no escaping it any longer. Uncle John had been one of them before, and he was one of them now. And his uncle had brought him here to help win football games—nothing more. He didn't want to believe that, but what reason was left to doubt it? Probably, too, his coming here had done a lot to encourage and revive the idea of recruiting outside players. In a way that was the most depressing thought of all.

Suddenly, he didn't want to talk about it any more. He said, "Excuse me, Uncle John. I have to do some schoolwork."

But his mind was too troubled for study. He kept thinking about it. And all at once a happier thought struck him. Suppose the team played great football Saturday, beat Cliffton decisively. That should help block Mr. Carruth's little scheme!

He was still thinking of that when they took the field Saturday afternoon at Tiger Stadium. He was thinking of the people in those packed stands—every seat taken despite the raw, cold day—who were expecting a Westland victory. For the papers all over the state had named Westland the favorite. Cliffton had a great record in the Northeast Region. They had routed strong East Dallas High 36–6 the previous week while Westland was having a bad day against Burk City. But Westland had better balance, the papers said, had met tougher opposition. They should win.

Scotty was thinking of what it could mean if they lost.

Then he had no more time to think, because the green-and-gold team was coming down the field with the kickoff.

They brought it to their own 29, and Westland got a taste of the famed Cliffton multiple offense. Mixing

T, wing-T, and spread, Cliffton moved sharply, piercing deep into Westland territory.

It was first down on the 18. The wingback went into motion to the left off the wing-T, and the defense surged over to meet him. Scotty held back, watching the right end. The end, loafing along, suddenly cut and sprinted—and Scotty knew he'd guessed right. The wingback stopped, passed. The end lengthened his stride to get under the ball.

Scotty cut it pretty fine. He snatched the ball on the tips of his fingers on a dead run. He slanted across field, reversed direction to elude one tackler. Two others were closing in. Brooks wiped one out with a lovely block. Scotty jolted the other with a straight-arm, skipped away, and he was gone—ninety-five yards in all for a touchdown.

The stands roared their delight. But the noise subsided a little when a Cliffton end deflected the kick. It was 6–0.

It settled down to a battle of stubborn defenses. Then early in the second quarter, Westland came up with the "big play." It was a simple pitchout, but everything clicked, faking and blocking. Scotty got outside the end and turned upstream. Hodges toppled the halfback, and that was it. Scotty sped seventy-four yards untouched.

On a tough decision Jeffers decided to go for the one point. Scotty kicked, and it was 13–0.

It happened soon after that. There'd been an exchange of punts, then another punt over the goal line by Cliffton. It was on the third play of the series.

Scotty was carrying on a trap. The tackle didn't take the bait. He filled the hole. Scotty dipped a shoulder and tried to wedge by. The tackle's lunge bumped him off balance. Another man hit him, then another—and everything went black. . . .

He awoke, conscious of a throbbing pain in his head.

"Okay, young man, just take it easy now."

It was Doc Roden, the team physician. Scotty saw now that he was in the dressing room, lying on a training table.

"What happened?" Scotty asked. "I been out long?"

"About five or six minutes," the doctor told him. "We brought you right inside. Your helmet got knocked off and you got a pretty heavy lick on the head. How are you feeling?"

"I feel okay. I can go back in the second half, can't I?"

The doctor didn't answer him.

Some fifteen minutes later he was sitting up, feeling much better. His head was clear of the fog now, though some of the ache was still there. The door opened; players started coming in. Scotty knew by their look it hadn't been going too well.

Jeffers came over, and Scotty said, "How are we doing, Coach? What's the score?"

"Thirteen to seven," Jeffers said. "They scored on us in the last minute."

Scotty frowned. That didn't sound good. "I'm feeling fine now, Coach. All ready to go." He had to get back in there!

Jeffers looked at the doctor. Doc Roden said, "It

might be like I told you and it might not, Lee. He seems okay, but . . . I guess it's up to you to decide."

The coach turned back to Scotty. "Doc thinks you may have a mild concussion. No more football for you today."

Scotty protested. "But, Coach—"

"I might send you in to kick a point-after. Nothing more." Jeffers' tone was one of finality.

As it turned out, Scotty wasn't needed to kick any points. Westland didn't score any more touchdowns in that game.

Cliffton did, however. They tallied on a long pass four minutes deep in the fourth quarter. They tried for two on a run. McGraw and Cowan spilled it. The score was 13–13.

Scotty sat on the bench, seeing his mates halted after a long drive, suffering the torture of being helpless to do anything about it. Now they had the ball again but were bogging down at midfield.

He looked at the clock. Five minutes. Scotty squirmed. What if the game ended in a tie?

Then he remembered. In case of a tie in the play-offs the decision went to the team that penetrated more times inside their opponent's 20-yard line. If penetrations were even, first downs decided it.

He looked down the bench. "What are penetrations now?"

"Four apiece," said one of the boys.

"How about first downs?"

"They're ahead of us, by about three."

He jumped to his feet. McGraw had just made a prodigious catch of a long pass as he was hit on the Cliffton 26-yard line.

The defense massed tight, knowing Westland would likely go for the penetration." It was almost a goal-line defense, leaving open an excellent opportunity for passes. But Westland did not pass. They burrowed out the yards. Cowan for two. Dave for one. Cowan for one. Still two yards short. Hodges sent Hanna, Scotty's replacement, wide on a pitchout. They slammed him out of the 19-yard line. Westland had its penetration!

The rest of the game kept the fans close to hysteria. Cliffton went to the spread and started passing. Two were overshot. But a third found its mark. An end took it and was almost loose when Hodges brought him down. The ball was on Westland's 25-yard line.

Now Cliffton went for the penetration, knowing their advantage in first downs. Four times they unleashed power into the line. On the fourth try, with a mere foot to go, the quarterback tried to sneak, and he was down under an avalanche even as he took the ball—still short of the 20-yard line!

The Tigers froze the ball for three plays, and the gun went off. By the narrowest of margins, Westland was in the state finals. . . .

It was about ten o'clock that night, and Scotty was at home in bed. He'd been there since his uncle had brought him home from the game. After talking to the doctor, his uncle had insisted that Scotty go home and get in bed and stay there. He'd even talked of calling a doctor to the house, but Doc Roden had assured him it was unnecessary.

"Just see that he stays quiet and rests," Doc Roden had said. "I'll give him a checkup in my office Monday."

The whole thing was unnecessary, Scotty thought. He'd gone off to sleep early and now he was wide-awake, sleepless.

He heard the rumbling of the garage door, then footsteps downstairs.

"Back so soon, John? It must have been a short meeting."

The door to Scotty's room was open and he could hear his aunt's voice quite clearly.

"Scotty asleep?" his uncle asked.

"Yes. Ever since you left."

"It wasn't exactly a meeting. King called a few men over for a powwow. I left early. I think if I'd stayed any longer I would have punched his big nose."

"Why, John— Why are you so angry?"

"Angry! I'm furious! Carruth was beefing about the game, blasting Jeffers. Among other things, he said Jeffers nearly lost the game by keeping Scotty on the bench the last half. I reminded him the boy was hurt— and you know what he said? 'We had a ball game to win,' he said. 'A little bump on the head! That's nothing for a tough little rooster like that kid.' I tell you, Alice, I could have slugged him! I told him this kid's health and safety meant a million times more to me than any ball game and that when Jeffers kept the boy out, that made Jeffers a man in my book. A real man.

A lot better man than those guys who don't care what happens to a boy so long as they can win a game—or a bet. If that bunch thinks I'd be a party to stabbing Jeffers—"

"Shh, John. Not so loud. You might wake up the boy."

"Aw, that kid sleeps like a log. I'm going to do something about this. Tomorrow I'm— Okay, I'll quiet down, but—"

Scotty heard no more. His aunt and uncle had wandered into the kitchen, and he could no longer hear what they were saying. But he was gladdened by what he had heard. Ashamed and glad at the same time. Ashamed of doubting his uncle. Glad he'd been so wrong. For days he'd been battling with himself—the loyalty he owed Uncle John against what he thought was right. Now there was no conflict at all. It was a wonderful feeling, as if a weighty burden had been lifted from him.

Before long he was sleeping—a sound, untroubled sleep.

He was sitting in the living room Sunday afternoon when Aunt Alice came in. A number of the team had been over to visit him during the afternoon. Also Esco and some fellows from electronics class. Now they'd left and Scotty was watching a TV program.

"Scotty, I must apologize," his aunt said. "I forgot to tell you a young lady called last night when you were asleep. She asked how you were feeling. Now what was her name? Jenny—no—"

"Julie Fisher?"

"That's it. I thought you might want to call her back."

"You bet I do!" Scotty grinned. "Thanks, Aunt Alice."

He hadn't seen much of Julie that fall. Hurried greetings in the halls—that was about all. He knew she had no "steady," but somehow he'd had the feeling Julie wasn't too interested in him. One thing he remembered, though. She'd acted the same toward him before and after he'd gained acclaim in football—no more friendly, no less.

He dialed her home and was glad to hear her voice answer.

"My aunt told me you called to inquire about the casualty," he said. "Thought I'd tell you he's going to live."

"Good." A pleasant laugh came over the wire. Then, seriously, "I talked to some of the boys at church today. They said you weren't badly hurt. Is that right, Scotty?"

"Just addled my noggin for a few minutes. Nothing much."

"That's good to know. Will you be able to play Saturday?"

"Sure will. Doc says just take it easy first couple of workouts and I'll be ready to go."

"Well, you be good and do what the doctor says. Glad you called."

"Er— Julie"— Scotty swallowed and took the plunge —"I was wondering if you had a date for the football banquet."

"No, Scotty, I don't have."

"Would you—I mean I'd sure like to have you go with me."

"Thanks, Scotty. I'd be glad to. Do you know where it's to be held?"

"I think— I'm not sure—" he stammered. She'd accepted, just like that! He recovered his voice. "I don't think they've decided yet. But I'll be seeing you at school."

Julie was silent a moment, as if she were waiting for him to say more. Then she said, "Be seeing you then. 'Bye."

Scotty racked the phone, wishing he could have thought of something more to talk about.

Anyway, that banquet was going to be a nicer occasion now. Much nicer. Only one thing more was needed to make it a perfect evening—a championship trophy on the speakers' table.

"I understand you boys have been holding secret practice all week. Cooking up some special medicine for Concho?"

"Come in, Uncle John." It was Friday night. Scotty was reading an English assignment, trying to get his mind off the game for a while. So far, he hadn't succeeded very well. "We've been working on something," he added, answering the question. "Not allowed to tell what it is, of course."

"Team feeling good? Think you're going to win?"

Scotty said with quiet emphasis, "We're not riding that plane to Dallas to lose a ball game."

Officials of the two schools had not been able to come to terms on a home site for the game, and neither would consent to having it decided by the toss of a coin. As a compromise, they had accepted the invitation from Dallas to play in the Cotton Bowl Stadium.

"Well, I'm sure glad you're in top condition again." His uncle gave him a sober look. "Most folks think you boys haven't got a chance, Scotty."

"We know, Uncle John."

They knew, indeed. For a town whose team was in the state finals, Westland was strangely unhappy. "What's wrong with the Tigers?" was the question heard everywhere. Were those reports really true? Was there dissension on the team? And look at what Concho had done last week. They'd swamped DelVerde 34–7.

The local papers were pessimistic. Even Carlton was fearful. Had the team gone stale? Could Jeffers bring them back by Saturday? As for Pinley, he saw nothing ahead but a defeat worse than the one suffered at the hands of the Raiders earlier in the season. He ridiculed Jeffers' strategy in the semifinal. Why go for the penetration instead of a score—when it would have been easy to pass? What if Cliffton had scored again? What if Cliffton had got one more yard on that last play, thereby winning on first downs? And above all, Pinley wailed, why had Jeffers kept Clayburn on the bench the entire last half? It was obvious he wasn't seriously hurt.

"We know," Scotty repeated. "But we may surprise them."

194

John Durham took a deep breath. "They're out to get your coach. Did you know that?"

Scotty nodded. He was glad it was "they," not "we." "It's a shame, Uncle John, the town letting those men who bet big money dictate—"

"Don't stop, kid. Go on and say it. You're right. They are gunning for one of the finest men and greatest coaches in the business, and betting has a lot to do with it. I've had my eyes opened to what it can do, Scotty. How it can make an otherwise decent man willing to risk a boy's whole future so they can win a buck on a ball game. And so they can brag too. That's part of it." He paused, hesitating over the next words. "You know, I guess I never saw it before. That is, I never had a son of my own. . . . And, well, you've sort of become like a son to me, Scotty."

Scotty swallowed a tight feeling in his throat. "Thanks, Uncle John. You make a pretty swell dad too."

John Durham laughed to cover up his embarrassment. "Do you want to know something, Scotty? I'll never bet anything bigger than a Stetson hat again on a ball game. I'm cured—"

"Telephone, John," Alice Durham called.

Scotty returned to his assignment, "The Revolt Against Classicism in Poetry." He had waded doggedly through about a page when his uncle came back.

"That was King Carruth." John Durham gave Scotty a long look. "I might as well tell you what I've been doing this week, Scotty. I've been talking to a lot of people. I've organized a citizens' committee for the support of Jeffers."

Scotty brightened. "Gee, that's great, Uncle John."

"Our committee talked to Frank Blake, the board chairman, yesterday, and he promised to hear them at the next regular board session. I'm—well, you might say I started the thing. King knows who's behind it, and is he sore! He gave me an ultimatum to call off my dogs. He said he'd beat me, no matter what I tried."

Scotty said, "Do you think Mr. Carruth—those men —can really get Coach fired?"

His uncle was thoughtful. "They can make it tough. King has influence. And he has prepared his ground well."

"But what if we beat Concho and win the championship?"

"I'd guess King will suddenly discover he was 'misled and misinformed' and would try to hop on the victory wagon."

"Then," Scotty said, "the thing we have to do is get out there tomorrow and beat Concho."

His uncle smiled. "That would be a good start toward getting the situation cleared up, I think."

Chapter
Twenty

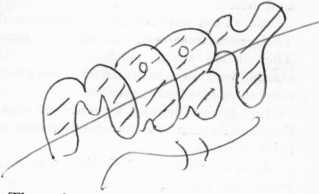

The early morning fog had lifted, and the giant Bowl was flooded with sunlight. The air was crisp and free of wind. More than fifty thousand people were already seated in the double-deck stands, and they were still coming in. It was the largest crowd ever to witness a Texas schoolboy final.

The Concho team had drawn them there—the fabulous, unbeaten Scarlet Raiders whose touchdown terrors, Wingo and Rawdon, had ripped like a tornado through all opposition. From all over north and central Texas, fans had come to see this team, called by many the most awesome high-school football machine in the state's history.

They had only one fear, these neutral fans—that the

game wouldn't be much of a contest. Still, Westland had a pretty fair little team. Maybe they'd make it worth watching.

The partisan fans were there too. Five thousand from Concho, noisy and confident. Four thousand from Westland, holding to a tiny thread of hope—hope for a miracle.

The Tigers were deploying to receive the kickoff. Their faces were marked with grim determination. They hadn't talked much today. But they'd said enough. Back there in the dressing room they'd quickly come to an agreement: they were dedicating this game to Lee Jeffers. Simply, without any demonstration, they'd made their vow to each other—to win this game for their coach.

Down the field, the line of Scarlet Raiders stood poised and confident. They'd beaten this team once already and they could do it again. They had no doubt about it.

The whistle blew. The Scarlet line moved forward. The ball soared high and deep. Scotty took it on the goal line and hurried upfield. Cowan toppled one man, McGraw another, and a lane opened. Scotty sprinted. The lane closed, filled with red jerseys. They rode him down on the 34-yard line.

The customers didn't have to wait long for their first thrill. On the first play, as Hodges faked to Cowan, Peninger bruised in from his defensive end, rushing the quarterback. Hodges pitched out. Scotty took it, and Dave, relieved of his block on Peninger, went for Emery, the halfback. It worked with the perfection of a picture play. Dave's block was a thing of beauty. Sanchez, pulling out from guard, was down fast, harassing safety-man Wingo just enough. Scotty breezed through a vast and beautiful expanse of open space—all the way to the end zone.

The noise in the stands abated suddenly. Scotty turned, feeling a horrible premonition. He saw the referee's gesture. An infraction by Westland. The score did not count.

They were penalized five yards for backfield in motion. Dave, the offender, shook his head sorrowfully. "Forget it," Scotty consoled. "Keeping blocking like that and we'll get it back."

First and fifteen now. Hodges said, "Let's fool 'em. Do it again. Same play."

But the rhythm wasn't there this time. Scotty, a little ahead of the pitchout, had to break stride trying to get away from Peninger's rush.

And he never quite got possession of the ball. He was still clutching at the elusive leather when Peninger hit him. The ball shot free. A scarlet jersey covered it on the 24.

The Raiders hammered the line. Rawdon, then Emery, then Wingo, the speedster, cutting inside end to the 15. Murphy at quarterback sneaked for the first down. Concho kept slashing into the fighting wall of Tigers, carving out small but precious yardage. Then they sent Wingo wide—into the open. Scotty hurled himself like a projectile. But Wingo's flying feet were already past the flag.

The place kick was good, and Concho led 7–0.

A little more grim but no less determined, the Westland players deployed again to receive. Nobody was blaming anybody. But they knew they couldn't afford many mistakes like that.

Cowan took the kickoff to the 29, and they started a drive. But it was heavy going. They were up against some of the state's greatest defensive stalwarts—rugged, aggressive Burkett; Dulin, a mammoth block of granite; Peninger, an agile mauler; bull-like Rawdon; Weimar, tough, crafty middle backer. Yet Westland moved the ball. Two key plays, a 14-yard crossbuck by Scotty and a spot pass to McGraw, kept the drive alive.

Then on second and two, Hodges elected to pass. It was sound strategy, with Concho forced to play it tight. Hollum, crossing over from left end, jumped for it crossing the goal line. The ball teetered off his fingers—just enough for Wingo to grab it and scamper out to the 30. So for the second time a break had thwarted Westland's bid.

The Raiders varied their attack now. Power slants, dive plays, pitchouts, crossbucks, a pass here and there. It was a beautiful exhibition of precision football, and the neutral fans and the Concho crowd enjoyed it immensely.

The Tigers fought to stem the tide. Down inside the 20 they dug in. They stopped Rawdon. They halted Wingo on a sweep. Ball on the 14, third and seven. Murphy faked to his fullback, Rawdon, and passed. Dave knocked it down. Fourth and seven.

The Westland fans groaned. A flag was down, and

the referee was stepping off five yards. Offside! Back to third down now—and only two yards to go.

The Raiders used trickery. A fake to Wingo, a lateral to Rawdon. The big fullback came tearing around end. Dave had an arm on him, lost him. Then Scotty hit him, and Rawdon went down like a felled tree. He got up, blank surprise on his face. Then he said, "You'll kill yourself off for nothing, little man. We're going to score anyway."

They did. With four downs to make three yards, they used deception with a double handoff. For just an instant a tiny gap opened off tackle, and Wingo skittered across. Their conversion made it 14–0.

Concho fans were going wild. Westland supporters sat in glum silence. Among the rest of the crowd there was much head shaking. It was looking too one-sided to be interesting.

The Tigers huddled briefly. Hodges said, "Okay, they've had their luck and shot their bolt. Now let's get some tallies for our side."

"On this kickoff," McGraw said almost fiercely, "everybody get his man!"

The kick went to Scotty. As he raced up the middle he saw a wondrous thing happening in front of him. Scarlet jerseys were toppling like tenpins. He found his lane, burst out into open ground, blazed past two opponents, sprinted a tightrope down the sideline with only Wingo in pursuit. Wingo closed the gap. Around the 20, he made his bid, leaping like a catamount. Scotty veered slightly, and Wingo hit the grass empty-handed. Scotty crossed the goal line. Thousands joined the Westland stands in a noisy demonstration.

Scotty's kick was straight and true. It was 14–7.

Concho consumed five full minutes in a slow, plodding advance. Their obvious strategy was to keep possession, score late in the period, leaving Westland little time before the half.

The Tigers halted them on the 17. Westland had four minutes and 83 yards to go. They went to work. Scotty got six on a pitchout, shot a running pass to Cowan for nine more. Dave picked up three on a counter, Cowan six on a dive. Scotty faked a running pass, kept, and threaded through a broken field to the Concho 48. Another running pass was in Hollum's hands, but Emery hit him hard and he dropped the ball. Cowan and Scotty netted nine on two plays. Fourth and a yard. Hodges tried to sneak for it, but the giant Dulin smothered him. The ball went over.

The clock was on its last minute. Wingo scurried wide. McGraw bumped him, and Wingo fumbled the ball. He scrambled for it, got it, and turned to see McGraw and Cowan bearing down on him.

Whether it was a stroke of inspiration or a wild impulse, no one ever knew. Wingo backed up and threw the ball. He simply slung it downfield as far as he could throw. And Peninger, loitering down there, picked up speed suddenly. His ground-eating stride carried him under the flying leather. He picked it out of the air and ran over the goal line. The Concho fans were deliriously happy.

A pall settled over the Westland stands. Concho's

failure on a pass for two points gave them no consolation. Time had run out on the last play, and their team trailed 20–7.

The three-minute buzzer sounded. The dressing room was quiet as the players waited for Jeffers to speak.

His tone was calm, deliberate. "All right, men, you know what we're going to do this half. If we should have started it sooner, I'll take the blame. I had reasons, of course. Mainly, that Concho could chart no defense at halftime. That last score of theirs made the odds a little tough. But I want you boys to know I'm proud of your performance. The ball took some pretty bad bounces for you. But the breaks have a way of evening up—for a team that keeps fighting. And this thing will work. Let's make it work!"

There was no demonstration as they filed out. Each man was busy thinking about his part in the job ahead. . . .

The kickoff went to Wingo, and they swarmed to meet him. Then, in sudden dismay, they realized Wingo didn't have the ball.

They'd fallen for the old crisscross again! Perhaps they'd instinctively expected Wingo to keep. Maybe they'd been too eager. Anyway, there was Murphy, speeding past two of them, breaking into the clear, with only Scotty between him and the goal line—and two blockers still ahead!

Scotty gave ground, dancing, weaving, making himself an elusive target. One blocker sliced at him, and he skipped away. Murphy cut to utilize the other blocker. Scotty threw out a hand, using the blocker's helmet as a fulcrum, pivoting. He was two strides behind Murphy, pursuing. Now one stride. He drove into Murphy's flying legs, and Murphy hit the ground skidding. The ball was on Westland's 29-yard line.

The Tigers came down, something like awe in their faces. Dupre said, "That's the greatest piece of defensive play I ever saw."

McGraw boomed, "Are we going to waste it—or are we going to stop these gorillas!"

They gave him the answer without delay. They stacked Rawdon at the line of scrimmage. Cowan shot the gap and pitched Wingo for a loss. Murphy was stopped dead on the option play. Concho, trying to hit the coffin corner, punted out on the 16.

The Tigers lined up. And a wave of startled comment rippled through the stands.

It was a spread. But what a spread! The ends were split nearly ten yards out. Cowan and Franklin were positioned as halfbacks in the two big slots between tackle and end. Tackle to tackle, the line was tight. Two yards back, right of center, was Hodges. And some five yards back, looking very much alone, stood Scotty Clayburn.

Comment in the stands had one refrain: Only one man back there to get the ball. They'd murder him!

The diagnosis was not quite accurate. Hodges could also take the snap, carry on a quick opener, or feed off to a man in motion. But the first snapback did go to Scotty. In fact, in this new offense fashioned the past week, it would go to him on almost every play.

He swung out as if to run, faded a little, and flipped a pass down the middle. Cowan, wide open, took the ball and ran another eight yards before they knocked him off his feet.

The next play started the same way. The secondary sagged to cover receivers. Two linemen broke through, rushing Scotty. Hodges laid a block on one of them, and Scotty took off through the wide hole inside end. He rambled to midfield.

He faded again. Scarlet jerseys were pouring through. He slid away from one, spurted forward to elude another. He ran laterally a moment, stopped, sidestepped another tackler. At last he found what he was looking for—a man open. He threw. The ball settled gently into McGraw's hands, thirty-five yards away. McGraw swiftly conveyed it across the goal line.

Deaf to the clamor in the stands, Scotty kicked very carefully. The score became 20–14.

On the kickoff the Raiders tried the crisscross, and it fooled nobody. Wingo was clobbered on the 25. Concho moved the ball. But their attack seemed to have lost some of its precision. It sputtered out at midfield. They kicked over the goal line.

Hodges tried a quick opener, but Dulin would not be moved. Scotty took over the show again. He ran twice and passed three times for two completions, and Westland was on Concho's 45.

Then Concho came up with a new maneuver. They moved Peninger over to right end and sent him buzzing in fast. Obviously, he was assigned to rush

Clayburn at all costs. Scotty managed to evade him and to complete a shot to Hollum for eleven yards. But the next time the speed of the big end's rush was more than Scotty had reckoned with. Peninger dumped him for a seven-yard loss.

Peninger grinned at him. "You've had your fun for the day, chum. We've got that silly formation figured now."

In the huddle Scotty said, "I guess it's about time we serve up our dose for that crashing end."

He took the snap from center. Again Peninger came pouring in. Scotty pushed a little shovel pass to Hodges as the quarterback moved laterally. Hodges ran wide. Peninger wasn't there. Neither was anybody else. Hodges swept nineteen yards before Wingo hauled him down. The ball was on the 22.

The Raiders called time out. Zerner, their coach, sent in a sub. There was a long consultation in the Concho huddle.

Play was resumed. Hodges drifted down the line again, just as before. This time Burkett came charging through recklessly, and Peninger floated over to cover Hollum. Weimar, from middle backer, stormed over to cover Burkett's charge.

Dave moved swiftly. His reverse body block nailed Burkett inside. Scotty kept the ball and sprinted into the vast opening left on the Concho wing. Hodges laid a block on Weimar. Scotty, racing Murphy for the corner, cut back sharply and went over as Wingo's futile dive fell short. The score was tied at 20–20, and the stands were going slightly mad.

There was a sudden hush. Hodges took the snap and set the ball down in one smooth motion. Scotty kicked. The ball tumbled sweetly between the uprights. Westland was ahead 21–20.

Many in the crowd were wondering. For the first time this year the Raiders were behind in a ball game. Would they come roaring back now and prove their greatness?

Concho brought the kickoff to their own 26. And all at once they began to flounder. The split-second timing, the air of confidence were suddenly missing. A bad handoff spoiled the first play. Wingo juggled a pitch-out and barely recovered before McGraw nailed him. A long huddle cost them five yards. A forward pass sailed clear off the field of play.

The crowd had its answer. The once-fearsome Raiders were coming apart at the seams!

The Tigers let a wobbly punt die at midfield and lined up in the spread again. But this time the snap went to Hodges. Dave and Hollum double-teamed Burkett. Both guards pulled out, Dent going for the end, Sanchez for the backer. Peninger fought past Dent, bearing down on Hodges. In that instant Hodges pitched out to Scotty, who breezed into a beautiful expanse around end—all the way to the Concho 27.

The next play started exactly the same way. But when the end penetrated deep, Hodges kept the ball and went for eleven more yards. While the Raiders were trying to figure that one out, Scotty took the ball wide again. Feinting a pass, he turned downfield behind a terrific block by Dave. Emery hurtled him out two yards short of the goal. The Raiders massed in a nine-man line. They poured through, burying Scotty. But not before he'd lobbed a little pass to Cowan in the end zone. An explosion of sound rocked the stadium. Scotty kicked, and it was 28–20.

That was the beginning of the end. Concho tried to rally. They even managed two slogging drives. But their efforts were the efforts of defeated men—wavering, desperate, then frantic. Rawdon was ejected from the game for slugging. Wingo was taken out by his coach for fumbling on a key play—and there before the watching thousands Zerner berated him with angry gestures.

Westland's fifth touchdown came on a long crossfield pass, Clayburn to McGraw. Then, with the closing minutes ticking away and a short-range barrage carrying the Raiders downfield in one last aerial flare, a pass went astray. And it was Dave Franklin—the boy who never got in on the spectacular plays—who snatched it and ran eighty long yards for a touchdown.

For the first time, Scotty's kick was wide. The score was 41–20. Moments later, as a Concho pass fell harmlessly to the turf, the gun went off.

The Tigers from Westland were state champions.

Escaping, finally, from the delirious crowd that poured out onto the field, Scotty and his mates were filing through the exit toward the dressing room.

Scotty felt a tug on his arm. "Uncle John! Like the game?"

John Durham grinned widely. "Greatest I ever saw!

The way you kids came back and panicked 'em with that spread!"

They both halted in sudden surprise. Just outside the dressing-room door stood King Carruth.

"What are you doing here, King?" John Durham grinned. "I thought you'd be trying to get out of town."

Red-faced, Carruth said, "Now don't start ragging me, John. When I'm wrong, I'm the first to admit it. I'm trying—" He looked at Scotty. "Great game, kid. Great." Then he turned back to Durham. "I'm trying to get in there right now to see Jeffers. They say nobody but players can come in for fifteen minutes. As chairman of the athletic committee, I'm recommending a long-term contract—"

"King," John Durham said, "I don't think you're going to be chairman when you get home. I talked to Frank Blake today before the game. He said that after *my* committee talked to him, he had some personal talks with board members. Sort of polled their sentiments. It seems they all decided—before the game, mind you—they'd been about to make a big mistake. I reckon they're really sure of it now."

Carruth smiled feebly. "I agree. I agree. As chairman—"

"I'm trying to tell you. Frank said he's dissolving your so-called athletic committee at the next board meeting."

Carruth croaked hoarsely, "Surely he's not blaming me. Somebody gave me a bum steer. I was misinformed—"

"You'd better think of a better story than that, King, before you get back to Westland. Some folks are going to remember for a long time that they were about to fire a coach who won them a state championship. More important, others will remember that he refused to play an injured boy, even though it might have cost him the championship and his job."

John Durham turned away in disgust from the sputtering Carruth. "Go on in and celebrate with your buddies, Scotty. When you get through, we're going to drive downtown for the biggest steak dinner you ever saw."

Around the gaily decorated banquet tables at the Hacienda Hotel sat the members of the football squad and their dates. At the center of the speakers' table one object dominated the scene. It was a full-size gold football, mounted on a tall silver column—the State Championship Trophy.

Two weeks had passed since that heart-stopping afternoon in the Cotton Bowl. Tonight Westland was giving its heroes the official tribute.

Now the gala evening—filled with speeches, applause, stories, reminiscences, laughter—was drawing toward a close. There was a short burst of applause as Clint Carlton of the *Times* rose to his feet. Then a hush settled over the room. This was the event everyone had been waiting for.

Scotty had found it difficult to listen to all that the speakers had said. Julie—buoyant and jolly, dressed in something lacy and blue, and looking very pretty indeed—had attracted much of his attention. Also, his mind had been straying back over the multiple events of the past few days.

He was going to college on a scholarship. It was settled. Mr. Bechtel had received assurances from the dean at Bryce Institute of Technology. There, Mr. Bechtel had told him, he would receive training equal to any in the country. And they had a football team. Not one of those come-only-if-invited teams, but a good, well-coached team, the teacher had said. It was all very wonderful. He would always be grateful to Mr. Bechtel.

And to Uncle John. His uncle had found a job for Scotty's mother in the alterations department of an exclusive dress shop in Westland. She could make a comfortable living while Scotty was away at college. She'd consented to sell the old house in Mayville and buy a little place Uncle John had spotted for her in Westland. Wally had "grown up a lot," she'd said, and could look after Ann and Charles in after-school hours until she got home from work each day.

And Uncle John's citizens' committee had expanded into a permanent organization. They had drawn up a constitution pledging members "to support the policies of school authorities and to help to promote better understanding between the coaches and fans."

". . . and it gives me great pleasure," Clint Carlton was saying, "to present these awards."

He was speaking of the trophies presented each year by the *Times*. Scotty wondered idly if the *Express* would sponsor some kind of an award next year to regain public favor. The *Express,* it seemed, had been bombarded with so many angry letters that the managing editor had discharged Spinks Pinley.

Carlton was saying, "These awards, you understand, are decided by a secret ballot of the team members. The boys pick their own stars." He held up a handsome trophy. "And now first, to the Best Lineman—that great tackle who for two years has been an anchor in the forward wall—Harry Dupre!"

Amid applause, Dupre walked up to receive the trophy. Haltingly, finding words difficult, Harry thanked the team.

"And now to the Best Blocker—a lion-hearted fellow who made the team the hard way—Dave Franklin!"

Choking with emotion, Dave tried to tell the audience there were others who deserved the award more. Applause drowned his words.

"And now, finally, to that lad who has thrilled all of us so many times—who has taught us all over again the true meaning of spirit and sportsmanship—the Most Valuable Player award—to Scotty Clayburn!"

The cheers were like a roll of thunder.

Scotty found himself holding a large and beautiful silver trophy. The sound subsided. They were waiting for him to speak. But words did not come easily. His heart was too full of things he could not put into words. Things about Westland High, where he had found new friends and a new future. About this team—the greatest bunch of fellows in the world.

Finally he found his voice. "I appreciate the honor symbolized in this trophy. But no man can be the most valuable player by himself. He's got to have a team with him. And I had a great one."

The cheers rolled out again. Why, he wondered, were his eyes getting misty? He was sure that he'd never been happier than he was tonight.

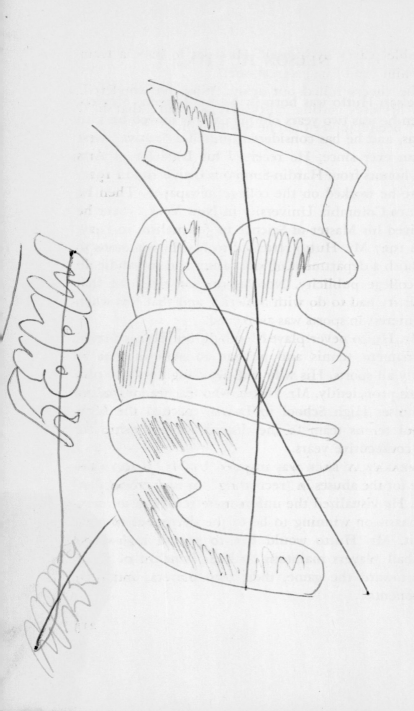

...to his...

When he was two years...
Texas and he has considered himself...
Texas licence. He received his doctorate in 1948
with honors from Martin...
where he worked on the ... group(?). Then he
received ... Columbia University in...
received the Master...

In 1957, he joined...
retired a position...
the college position...
under ... he had to do with...
his interest in space was...

Mr. Brown...
to complete ... six...
which all of...
technologically. All of...
at Santa ... School...
stored to the...
the consecutive years.

Brown's interest...
tests to the absolute necessity...
bed. He visualized the unbearable...
characteristic of having to leave the...
goal. At the same time to...
instead of water...
represented the same...
into life.

NELSON HUTTO

Nelson Hutto was born in Nuevo Laredo, Mexico. When he was two years old his parents moved back to Texas, and he has considered himself a "native" west Texan ever since. He received his Bachelor of Arts with honors from Hardin-Simmons University in 1925, where he worked on the college newspaper. Then he went to Columbia University in New York, where he received his Master of Science in Journalism in 1927.

In 1927 Mr. Hutto returned to Hardin-Simmons to establish a department of journalism and to handle all the college publicity. Needless to say, much of that publicity had to do with athletics, and that was when his interest in sports was awakened.

Mr. Hutto never played football, but he has played tournament tennis and he has an avid interest in nearly all sports. His wife and two daughters also play tennis proficiently. Mr. Hutto, who teaches journalism at Sunset High School in Dallas, coached the high-school tennis team to the district championship for five consecutive years.

BREAKAWAY BACK was inspired by Mr. Hutto's distaste for the abuses in "recruiting" for high-school football. He visualized the unfortunate results of an over-emphasis on winning to be to the detriment of t spirit. Mr. Hutto would like to see all high-s football players maintain "a high standard of rity toward the game, their own players, and opponents."

3 50 14
4

20

12 7 6
10 5
12 26

22
15 14

32

39 40

5

45